No
FEAR

ANNE SCHRAFF

SADDLEBACK
EDUCATIONAL PUBLISHING

2/13.

URBAN UNDERGROUND

SADDLEBACK
EDUCATIONAL PUBLISHING
www.sdlback.com

© **2011 by Saddleback Educational Publishing**
All rights reserved. No part of this book may be reproduced in any form or by any means, electronic or mechanical, including photocopying, recording, scanning, or by any information storage and retrieval system, without the written permission of the publisher.

ISBN-13: 978-1-61651-268-2
ISBN-10: 1-61651-268-7
eBook: 978-1-60291-993-8

Printed in Guangzhou, China
1010/10-25-10

16 15 14 13 12   1 2 3 4 5

CHAPTER ONE

Ernesto Sandoval, a sixteen-year-old junior at Cesar Chavez High School, was talking to the girl he desperately wanted to date, Naomi Martinez. They were standing by the colorful mural in front of the school. Naomi had just broken up with her long-time boyfriend, Clay Aguirre. Ernesto was slowly, awkwardly trying to make his move. It was Friday, and Ernesto needed to ask Naomi out before the weekend.

"This guy, Oscar Perez," Ernesto was explaining, "I heard him sing at a party at Carmen's house, and he was great. I thought maybe you'd enjoy—" Ernesto stopped talking because Naomi had stopped listening. She had turned and was watching Clay Aguirre arrive on campus. A cold chill went through Ernesto's body. *She still loved Clay.*

Naomi and Clay had been friends for a long time, ever since elementary school. They had dated seriously in high school. Clay had often been rude to Naomi, but she put up with his attitude because she loved him. Then they had had a big argument, and Clay punched Naomi in the face. She broke up with him then and there. Since then, he'd gone missing from Chavez, but this morning he was coming back to classes.

Clay's dark eyes fixed immediately on Naomi and Ernesto. Before the couple had broken up, Clay had been jealous of Ernesto. He'd feared Ernesto had his eye on Naomi, and he was right. Ever since coming here from Los Angeles with his family a few months ago, Ernesto had been drawn to the beautiful violet-eyed girl with the shiny black hair. In addition to being lovely, she was sweet and kind. Ernesto thought about her a lot, and he fantasized from the start about their being together someday. Once Clay had become so angry that he cornered Ernesto on a remote campus spot to warn him to stay away from Naomi.

"So," Naomi interrupted Ernesto's thoughts, "what were you saying about that singer, Ernie?"

Ernesto was going to suggest that he and Naomi go to the park on Sunday where Oscar Perez was giving a concert. There would be a lot of little bands and food booths as well. But the sight of Clay had made him tongue-tied. "Uh, I was just saying," he stammered, trying to ignore Clay, who was standing a few yards away glaring at him. "This dude, Oscar Perez, is gonna sing at the park Sunday, and it's sort of a festival. He's real good, and the food'll be good too. I just thought if you had nothing better to do, we could go over there, you know, and hear some hot music. We could have some tacos and chips and salsa too."

"That sounds nice, Ernie," Naomi surprised him by saying. But even though she was smiling, Ernesto could tell she was tense. She had loved Clay Aguirre for a long time, and maybe she still did. When Clay struck her, she was shocked and angry. She told him she never wanted to see him again. He apologized and pleaded with her to forgive him, but she stood her ground, at least at the time.

Ernesto hoped against hope she would continue to stand her ground. Yes, Ernesto hoped to get close to her. But even if she never wanted to date him, he cared for her as a human being. He hoped she knew that she owed it to herself to end the relationship with Clay. When a guy hits a girl, Ernesto believed, he's saying that this is the beginning, not the end, of a pattern of abuse. Ernesto cared about Naomi, and he didn't want her going down that frightening, painful road. He didn't want her hurt again. She didn't deserve to be hurt. No girl did.

"Okay then," Ernesto confirmed. "I'll pick you up about two in the afternoon."

"Good," she agreed.

Ordinarily, Ernesto would have been on top of the world. Naomi Martinez had actually agreed to go someplace with him! It was a date—exactly what he'd been hoping for and dreaming of. But seeing Clay Aguirre, with pure hatred boiling like volcanic lava from his eyes, stole the joy from the moment.

Before Naomi started walking toward English, she turned briefly in Clay's direction. "Hi Clay," she called. "I'm glad you're back in school." Then she walked on.

She was determined to be polite to him. She didn't hate him. She didn't think she could ever hate him, even though he had hurt her deeply. The black eye he gave her had hurt a lot, but the wound in her heart was much deeper and more painful. She had given her heart to him, and she had trusted him. She had never thought he would hit her, and, when he did, he broke her heart. All her dreams about their future together crashed to her feet like shattered crystal. All the wonderful memories of their times together mocked her now.

5

When Naomi was out of sight, Ernesto started for Ms. Hunt's English class. They were starting to study *Oedipus Rex* in the drama unit. It was a Greek tragedy, a horrible tale of human suffering, shame, and guilt.

"It was all your fault, you know, Sandoval!" Behind Ernesto, Clay's sharp voice penetrated the warm autumn air like a knife.

Ernesto tried to ignore him. But the other boy came up alongside him and spun around to face him. "You messed up the best thing I ever had," Clay Aguirre accused him face to face. "I love Naomi so much. I always loved her. But that night when she was saying how ripped you looked, one thing led to another. I got so mad. I knew you were trying to take her from me. I was just crazy with fear that you'd succeed, Sandoval. I don't know why I hit her. I never hit her before. I never would again. But she took it so hard. She dumped me, man."

Ernesto tried to be reasonable. "Aguirre, it wasn't my fault. It was your fault. It's an awful thing for a guy to hit a girl. You did it, man. It had nothing to do with me."

"Now you're movin' in on her, just like you wanted," Clay snarled bitterly. His voice was raspy with rage. "She's weak and sad. She's vulnerable, easy pickin's for a nobody like you. She'd never go for a wimpy jerk like you if she was herself."

Ernesto pushed past him, walked on, and joined a crowd of students. In the group were his best friend, Abel Ruiz, and two guys from his track team, Julio Avila and Jorge Aguilar.

"I see old Aguirre is back," Abel noted with a shudder. "Be careful, man. Better steer clear of Naomi for a while. She's poison, dude, with that creep on the prowl."

"I'm not gonna let fear rule my life," Ernesto declared, showing more bravado than he felt. As the group moved toward the school building, Ernesto recalled a incident of just a few weeks ago in the *barrio*. A gangbanger nicknamed Coyote shot and killed his ex-girlfriend's new boyfriend. Coyote was so angry when his girlfriend ditched him for another guy that he killed the new guy, Tommy Alvarado. The gang-banger stalked Yvette Ozono to her own sixteenth birthday party and took down Tommy right in front of her. That story was in the back of Ernesto's mind, but he didn't really think Clay Aguirre was that dangerous.

"Me and Naomi are going to a festival in the park on Sunday," Ernesto announced, as he and Abel entered the building. "This guy Oscar Perez is performing, and he's a blast."

"Oh man!" Abel moaned. "You're playin' with fire, dude."

They reached Ms. Hunt's classroom. Naomi was already at her desk. Ernesto walked in and sat down, and then he saw Clay slip in the back door. Ernesto could feel the boy's hostile gaze boring into his skull. But Ernesto made up his mind he'd just ignore Clay.

Clay wasn't a good student. Now he had such a low grade point average that he'd lost his eligibility to play football, which he loved. He was at a really low place in his life. He couldn't play football, and he'd lost his girlfriend. Ernesto didn't feel sorry for him, though, because he'd brought it all on himself. Still, the guy had to be pretty torn up.

Toward lunchtime that day, Ernesto and Abel were looking for someplace to eat.

"Hey Ernie," Carmen Ibarra yelled. "You wanna each lunch with us?" She was sitting with Naomi and Yvette Ozono.

Ernesto's father, Luis Sandoval, taught history at Chavez High. He tried very hard to teach well and to influence his students to stay and graduate. But he also sometimes walked out into the *barrio* in the late afternoons and evenings and talked to dropouts, urging them to return to school. One of them was Yvette Ozono, who was with Naomi and Carmen Ibarra at lunchtime. Ernesto's father knew how insecure Yvette would be returning to school. So he enlisted two of his best and kindest students, Naomi and Carmen, to help her through the first days.

"Sure!" Ernesto called back. "Abel and I'll be right over."

The five of them sat down with their lunches under the eucalyptus trees. Yvette then looked at Ernesto and said, "I remember you. You were at Tommy's funeral with your father."

"That's right, Yvette," Ernesto acknowledged with a smile. "I'm so glad to see you back in school. There's nothing out there for kids who don't have a high school diploma. I mean, I got a little job at the pizzeria. But they won't even hire a kid there if you can't prove that you're still in school. No dropouts allowed, you know?"

"Yeah," Yvette affirmed, "that's what Mr. Sandoval told me. But it's scary coming back. My old boyfriend—Coyote—he talked me into dropping out. He kind of controlled me. I did everything he asked so he wouldn't get mad." A look of deep sadness passed through the girl's eyes like a shadow. "I thought Coyote loved me, even though he wasn't nice to me. I never knew what it was like to have a boyfriend who treated me with respect, you know, not until I met Tommy. And then . . ."

Naomi reached over and put her arm around Yvette's thin shoulders. Ernesto was impressed with her kindness. That was one of the things about her he found most endearing. Naomi was beautiful, and she wore the latest fashions. But her clothing didn't define her, as it did with some pretty, stylish girls. Naomi really cared about other people. "You'll be okay, Yvette," she said. "Tommy is in a better place now, and he wants you to have a good life."

"Yeah," Carmen chimed in. "Don't let the creeps win, my father always says. You'll have to meet my father sometime, Yvette. His name is Emilio Zapata Ibarra. When we have a party, he wears a plastic badge like a sheriff and a big hat. He can't stand the gangbangers and the dopers. He's a big guy and he goes after them. So they don't hang around our street, Nuthatch Lane, so much anymore."

A smile came to Yvette's face. If anybody could make a person smile, she could. Most of the time that Ernesto had seen Yvette, she looked inexpressibly sad. Now, with a smile, she looked lovely.

"You really live on Nuthatch Lane?" Yvette asked, giggling a little.

"Yeah," Carmen affirmed. "All the streets around here are named for birds. The guys who laid out the tracts thought that'd be a cute idea. I don't think I ever saw a nuthatch around here, though."

"I live on Bluebird Street," Naomi added, "but I never saw a bluebird there. All I see are big crows."

"We live on Starling Street," Yvette responded. "I don't know if I ever saw one of those."

They all laughed. Ernesto could see that Yvette was relaxing, becoming one of the gang. Dad's plan to make her feel at home was working.

Ernesto was finishing his sandwich. Then, out of the corner of his eye, he saw Clay Aguirre standing about a hundred feet away. He was standing by the vending machine. Maybe he was just trying to pick up something for lunch, but Ernesto thought he was there an awfully long time. Ernesto didn't want to turn and look straight at him. But he had the uncomfortable feeling that Aguirre was staring at Naomi.

"He's watching us," Abel remarked, knowing exactly what was going through Ernesto's mind. "He's watching you especially, Naomi."

"Oh, don't pay any attention to him," Naomi protested, but her voice shook a little. "He's having a hard time with this, but he'll get over it. I mean, you know, we were together for a long time."

Yvette looked up abruptly. A look of terror appeared in her eyes. "Naomi," she stammered, "di-did you just break up with your boyfriend?" She was visibly shaken. Ernesto knew what was going through the girl's mind—her relationship with Coyote and where that led. Coyote had been controlling and dangerous. He stalked Yvette after the breakup. When he saw her with another guy, he snapped and became a killer.

"Yeah," Naomi acknowledged, trying to appear very casual. "Clay and I have been close, but I decided to move on."

Ernesto and Abel exchanged worried looks. Yvette glanced over to the vending machine where Clay still stood, looking over in their direction. "He looks . . . *mean,*" Yvette commented nervously.

"He's not," Naomi assured her. "He just wants his own way." Her voice faltered. Ernesto wondered whether she was actually scared of Clay or rethinking breaking up with him. He couldn't tell, but she looked unhappy.

The bell rang, and they all moved on to their classes.

When Ernesto took a quick look over at the vending machine, Aguirre was gone. Ernesto breathed a sigh of relief. Aguirre just had to face reality. He had to get over Naomi. He'd blown it. He had to know in his heart that he had lost her through his own fault.

After classes that day, Ernesto noticed Naomi starting to walk home. He had his Volvo in the parking lot, and he hailed her. "Want a ride home, Naomi?"

Naomi shrugged. "I was going to walk home. It's a nice day. But why not?" She walked toward him.

They walked to the parking lot and Clay Aguirre was nowhere to be seen.

Clay was a good-looking guy—better looking than Ernesto, or so Ernesto thought. "I'm on the skinny side," Ernesto was thinking as he walked with Naomi. "For sure, Clay has a better build. I have to say I envy him when the chicks look in his direction a lot. Ah, a guy as handsome as Clay'll soon hook up with another girl. He won't have any problems finding one. Then Naomi'll be completely free. Maybe Clay even learned something in all this. You can't treat a girl badly man. Maybe he'll treat the next girl better. Naomi's put up with an awful lot of rudeness over the years."

As they turned down Bluebird Street, Naomi interrupted his thoughts. "What's that?"

"Some kind of van in your driveway, Naomi. You expecting a delivery?" Ernesto asked.

"Not that I know of," she said.

They got out of the Volvo and walked to the door. They could see Mrs. Martinez, Naomi's mother, holding a huge bouquet. She was smiling and saying, "Flowers! We got flowers! A dozen red roses!"

For just a second, Linda Martinez thought the roses were for her. Felix, her husband, was not a very sentimental man. But she'd just had a birthday, and he hadn't made anything of it. Maybe he remembered,

16

she hoped. Maybe these roses were a belated birthday present.

Brutus, the family's pit bull, was still barking at the delivery truck as it left the driveway. Mrs. Martinez, who used to be terrified of the dog, now commanded, "Hush up, Brutus. Don't go on so. You don't bark at somebody bringing roses. Oh, aren't they beautiful?"

Naomi smiled at her mother. Mom usually had a hard time with Dad, and a little gesture of love and appreciation from him was a rarity. Ernesto thought of the many times his own father brought home flowers or candy or even a little piece of jewelry for Mom—for no reason at all. His only reason was that he remembered how much he loved her. His presents always delighted Mom, and Ernesto loved his father for bringing them home.

Mrs. Martinez fumbled for the note in the box of flowers. She was so nervous she couldn't find it. "Why do they hide the notes?" she laughed. Her face was flushed. Even though she was in her forties, she looked almost schoolgirlish in her excitement.

"Who's there?" Felix Martinez yelled from inside the house. "Who's at the door? Linda, you said you were making me a cup of coffee. Where the devil is it? What are you doing at the door?" He sounded even angrier than usual.

Then the little card tumbled out from the red roses. It fell on the doorstep, and Linda Martinez stooped to pick it up with trembling hands. In her eagerness, she almost scratched herself on one of the rose thorns.

The smile that had been on her face vanished in an instant. "Oh!" she said in a faint voice. "Naomi, the roses are for you." As an afterthought, she forced a thin smile. "Somebody sent you roses."

"You gonna spend the whole day out there?" Mr. Martinez yelled. "Do I need to go down to the fast-food joint for a cup of coffee? A man works hard all day, and he can't even get his wife to make him a cup of coffee!"

"I'm coming, Felix," Linda Martinez responded, going into the house with Brutus at her heels.

Naomi took the card. She recognized Clay Aguirre's handwriting.

> Babe, please forgive me for what I did. I swear to you nothing like that will ever happen again. I miss you so much, Naomi. I can't sleep, and I can't eat. I don't want to lose you, Naomi. I'm hurting, babe. You won't return my calls. Just call me and let's talk. We can work this out. Call me. I love you, Clay."

A look of pain and sadness came over Naomi's face. Ernesto wanted to tell her to be strong, just to ignore the note and the roses. But he knew it wasn't his place to say such a thing. He had an ulterior motive. He wanted Naomi for himself. But to himself he whispered, "Girl, be strong. Don't weaken . . ."

Naomi stood there, looking at the roses. Each one was perfect. "He must have spent a fortune," she remarked in a broken voice. "Oh Ernie! *This is so hard . . .*"

CHAPTER TWO

By the time Ernesto got home, he had a message on the home phone's answering machine. "It's just too soon," Naomi said in the message. "Thanks for asking me, and it woulda been fun. But I think it'll be easier for me and Clay to get over our relationship if we don't hook up with anybody else for a while. Sorry, Ernie."

Badly disappointed, Ernesto plopped own on the sofa in the living room. His grandmother was watching a nature special on television with Ernesto's sisters, eight-year-old Katalina and six-year-old Juanita. Ever since *Abuela* came to live with Ernesto's family, she and the girls were in-separable. *Abuela*'s spending so much time with the girls freed Mom up so that she could finish her children's book. Now that it had been sold to a publisher, she had time to text back and forth to the illustrator about what the pit bull and the cat in the book would look like. As the illustrator made rough drafts, Mom looked at them on her computer. It was such an exciting time for Ernesto's mother. She loved being a wife and mother, but never until now was her personal life so compelling. Ernesto was happy for her.

But he felt really bad about Sunday. Ernesto drifted outside, to the yard.

Dad was sitting outside on a redwood bench, going over tests from his classes. As the natural light faded, he put the tests away and admired the starry skies. "I've finished grading my American history tests, and now I can admire the constellations," Dad told Ernesto with a smile.

Ernesto sat down next to his father on the bench. "You know, Dad," Ernesto confided, "me and Naomi were planning to go to that festival in the park Sunday. But when I brought her home from school today, she found a dozen red roses and this big, drippy note from Clay. He wants to get back with her."

Dad frowned and commented, "I hope she ignores it."

"No," Ernesto sighed, "she cancelled Sunday. She got this real sad look on her face when she read Clay's note. Then she told me how hard it was to break up with him. I think she's weakening, Dad."

"You can't do anything about it, *mi hijo*," Dad advised. "I know you care about the girl. I know you're worried about her, but it's a decision she has to make. Of course, it'd be a terrible mistake for her to go back with a boy who punched her in the face. But you've got to remember the family she comes from. Her father doesn't treat her mother with respect, and that's how Naomi has grown up."

"Naomi talked to me about that, Dad," Ernesto replied. "She said her father is rude and sometimes unkind to her mother, but he never hit her. That's what Naomi told me. She said that was one of the reasons she split with Clay. She said she didn't want to live in fear."

Dad looked away from the sky and pressed his fingers into his closed eyes. Then he looked at Ernesto. "What she told you was not entirely true, Ernie. She may think it's true, but it isn't."

"What isn't true?" Ernesto asked in alarm.

"That Felix Martinez never hit his wife," Dad explained. "It was before we moved to Los Angeles, around Christmas, when all the neighbors got together for a party. Felix had been drinking a lot. I don't know what triggered the argument, but he hit Linda. They called Padre Benito from Our Lady of Guadalupe Church. He arranged for Mrs. Martinez and the children to go to a shelter for a few days. Then Linda came home with the children, and they reconciled. Naomi was too young to remember, but the older boys remember I'm sure, Orlando and Manuel."

Ernesto felt sick. "Why did she come home?" he asked.

Dad sighed. "Breaking up a marriage when there are four children. Ernie, Naomi's mother never worked. She was very young when they were married. Felix has always supported her. She was frightened to be on her own in the world with the *niños*."

"I wonder if he ever hit her again," Ernesto asked.

"I don't know, Ernie," Dad admitted. "I'm sure he's come close. Orlando, the oldest boy, left home when he was seventeen after some big argument. He hated his father, probably because of what was going on in the house. He got out of there as soon as he graduated high school."

"Where's Orlando now?" Ernesto asked. "Maybe he could talk to Naomi and convince her she's making a big mistake to go back with Aguirre."

Dad shook his head no. "Orlando has been estranged from his family for a long time. We weren't here when he took off. But Emilio Ibarra told me the boy was forbidden by his father to ever come near the house again. It was a pretty big thing. Felix Martinez calls him 'my evil son.' There's another boy too, Manuel. He's about nineteen. They kicked him out of the house. I understand he's hanging around the *barrio* somewhere now. It's a tragic situation for families to break up like that."

"It's just that Naomi is such a great girl, Dad," Ernesto said. "You should have seen how she was helping Yvette today. She was a regular little mother hen. She deserves a decent life. If she takes Clay back, then she's like walking in her mother's footsteps. And that makes me feel so bad."

"Yes," Luis Sandoval acknowledged, "Linda Martinez has let herself be mistreated. The saying goes that what you allow you encourage. Linda has encouraged Felix to be unkind."

"Dad," Ernesto asked, "suppose you were in my place and you cared about a girl like Naomi. Would you just give up on it or would you keep on trying?"

"*Mi hijo,*" Dad answered softly. "I confess to you that I am answering as a father who wants the best life for his son. You are perhaps harming your own future by persisting. You are becoming involved with a girl who has already permitted herself to be rudely treated by a young man. I feel sorry for her as you do, but your happiness is more important to me. I think being with Naomi will only cause you pain"

"Well, thanks for being honest, Dad," Ernesto said, getting up.

In the late afternoon on Saturday, Ernesto found Dom Reynosa and Carlos Negrete painting their mural under the supervision of Ms. Polk. He stopped to admire the beautiful colors that were emerging. "Great job, you guys!" he told them as he approached them. Ernesto's father had gotten the boys to paint the mural on the blank wall of the science building. He did it because they were taggers and potential dropouts, and he wanted to keep them attending Cesar Chavez High School. The mural had given them a reason to stay in school. Ernesto's father struggled daily to keep kids from dropping out of school and from being sucked into the hopelessness of the streets.

"Yeah," Dom nodded, "thanks."

As the boys worked, another boy came down the sidewalk and stopped. "How come you dudes're painting pretty pictures here at school when you could be makin' money on the street?"

"Hey Damon!" Carlos greeted the boy. Carlos turned to Ernesto, "This is Damon Benes. He's a homie. We had a few business deals goin'."

"Good luck, suckers!" Damon called over his shoulder, laughing and walking on.

When Damon was gone, Dom made a comment. "Gotta admit one thing. That dude always has plenty money."

"He used to go to Chavez, right?" Ernesto asked.

"Yeah," Carlos responded. "He dropped out when he was a sophomore. Know what, Ernie? Lot of the homies are ticked off at your old man. They're mad 'cause he's always walking around messing with the street corner deals and stuff. They're sayin' teachers should stay in the classroom and leave the streets to home boys."

"When my dad was a kid around here," Ernesto explained, "he had two really good friends. They ended up bad because nobody cared enough to save them. One went to prison, and the other overdosed. Dad doesn't want that to happen to other kids if he can do something about it."

Then Ernesto asked the question he'd come over to ask. "You guys ever run into Manny or Orlando Martinez around here?"

Carlos and Dom looked quizzically at each another. Dom replied, "I never heard of no Orlando, but Manny is a wannabe gangbanger."

Ernesto felt the pit of his stomach turn cold, as if a lump of ice had fallen into it. Nodding his head in a silent thank-you, Ernesto headed over to Hortencia's restaurant and tamale shop. His father's youngest sister ran the restaurant, a successful business. Ernesto didn't feel like eating anything, but he wanted a soda. After greeting his aunt, he sat down on one of the stools. Then he recognized a familiar face next to him.

"Hey, you're Oscar Perez, that great singer I heard at Carmen Ibarra's party," Ernesto said.

Perez was a handsome six footer with long, curly, black hair and flashing eyes. He grinned and looked at *Tía* Hortencia. "You hear that, baby? I'm great. The boy here just said so."

Ernesto couldn't believe Oscar Perez was addressing his aunt, but there were no other girls around.

"Yeah baby!" *Tía* Hortencia chuckled. "Don't I always tell you you're great?" She leaned over and planted a kiss on the young man's cheek.

Ernesto was stunned—*Tía* Hortencia and this singer? Ernesto remembered his *Abuela* scolding her youngest daughter that she was in her early thirties and not yet married. Hortencia *did* say something about having a boyfriend who was a musician. But Oscar Perez—who was creating a buzz all over southern California?

"You're coming to the festival tomorrow, eh dude?" Oscar asked Ernesto.

"I was figuring to, but my girlfriend changed her mind, so now I don't know," Ernesto answered.

"Ah," Oscar laughed, "get another girlfriend!"

Hortencia added, "Oscar, this is my nephew, Ernesto. He's my brother's child." Ernesto and Oscar shook hands, and Oscar added a hand grip.

"Ernie, you gotta come," Oscar urged him. "It's gonna be so much fun. Carmen will come with you. You call her up, *muchacho*."

"Maybe," Ernesto replied, finishing his soda. He bid good-bye to his *tía*, said "It was nice meeting you" to Oscar, and walked out of the shop.

On his way home, he felt happy that his bright, bubbly *tía* had found such a cool guy. But he didn't feel like going to the festival if Naomi wasn't with him. He didn't even think it was fair to call Carmen. He liked Carmen as a friend. But she might think he liked her more than he did if he called her. It wasn't fair to use her just so that he could go to the festival.

In spite of what his father or mother had said, Ernesto could not get Naomi off his mind. He couldn't accept the fact that she would get back with Clay Aguirre. Clay wasn't right for her. If Clay was a good guy and Naomi just liked him better than she liked Ernesto, that would be fair enough. Ernesto wouldn't be happy, but he could accept her decision. But Aguirre was no good for Naomi. He was no good for any girl unless he changed a lot, and Ernesto didn't believe Clay could change in any way. Ernesto didn't think people changed all that much. As the saying went, "The leopard can't change its spots."

On his way home, Ernesto noticed a bunch of guys outside the deli. He didn't recognize any of them by name, but he'd seen them around. He used to see Carlos and Dom hanging with them sometimes. So he figured they were taggers, maybe gang wannabes, or—worse—gangbangers.

"Hey," one of them shouted, "you Sandoval's kid?"

The guy who yelled was tall with a shaved head. He was one of two guys with shaved heads and a lot of tattoos on their arms and shoulders. They probably thought that made them look tough. It did, Ernesto thought. Several Sandoval families lived in the *barrio,* including Dad's two brothers and their families.

"Which Sandoval?" Ernesto asked.

"The teacher," the tall guy answered.

"Yeah," Ernesto admitted.

"Listen, man," the tall guy advised, "you tell your father to keep his nose out of where it don't belong. We don't need him snooping around, you get my meaning?"

Ernesto didn't want to mix it up with these guys. For one thing, there were four of them. For another, they looked like they probably had switchblades or even guns. It seemed as though every punk on the street had a gun.

Ernesto didn't say anything. He just kept on walking. Then one of the guys called out to him. "I seen you with my sister."

Ernesto turned sharply. He stared at a gaunt young man with a haunting resemblance to Naomi, especially in his eyes. "Who's your sister?" he asked, afraid he already knew the answer.

"Naomi Martinez," the boy replied. He still looked vulnerable. He was still a kid. Maybe a year from now he'd be as hard and cold as the others, but right now he was still a boy. "She your chick man?"

"No," Ernesto responded, "but she's a friend."

"She won't have anything to do with me," Manny Martinez explained. "Our old man sees to that. But she's a good kid. Listen man, next time you see her, tell her Manny says 'Hi,' okay? You tell her that her brother says 'Hi.'"

Ernesto nodded. He wasn't surprised that Felix Martinez had a kid like Manny. It was sad, but not surprising. There was not a lot of love in that house. That Naomi was as she was, *that* was the surprise. That was the miracle.

Ernesto didn't know whether he would relay Manny's message to Naomi. She had enough on her plate. He didn't look like the kind of a brother who could do her any good. Maybe, Ernesto thought, he'd just let it go.

When Ernesto got home, he texted Naomi. Maybe she'd changed her mind about going to the festival tomorrow. Maybe, by some small chance, those dozen red roses had lost their power by now. Naomi didn't text Ernesto back. Ernesto thought about asking Carmen, but he didn't. He decided he wouldn't go to the festival.

After dinner on Saturday night, Ernesto sat with his parents at the dinner table. He announced, "Did you guys know *Tía* Hortencia is dating this new singer, Oscar Perez?"

Mom grinned. "She told us. She's so excited. He's really nice and down-to-earth. When they go dancing, they do the tango. She wears this beautiful red dress, and they're amazing."

"Have you met this guy, Ernie?" Dad asked.

"Yeah, Dad," Ernesto replied. "I talked to him at the tamale shop. He's pretty cool. I saw him sing at the Ibarra house, and I really liked him. In person, he's warm and funny."

"He's kind of a big shot," Dad commented, a look of concern on his face. "He travels around with a trio, and he's got big

35

plans for the future. His group is made up of Chicano musicians, a little bit like *Los Lobos*. *Los Lobos* is iconic now, mixing Mexican and American music. That's what Oscar does. I hope my little sister knows what she's in for."

"Hortencia is a strong girl," Mom affirmed. "She's got her eyes wide open. If Oscar Perez is for real, then she'll give her heart to him. If not, she'll just go along for the ride and have fun. You needn't worry about that girl, Luis."

A moment later, the family heard the crackling sound of crashing glass and a couple of thuds. Juanita screamed, and Katalina came running from *Abuela*'s room.

Luis Sandoval jumped up and went to the living room. Somebody had thrown a sizable chunk of concrete through the picture window. The concrete lay on the carpet, surrounded by shattered glass. Ernesto's father threw open the front door and looked down the street. He hoped the culprits were still there, driving or running off, but no one was in sight.

"Luis, be careful!" Mom cried. "Don't go charging down the street!"

"I didn't hear a car," Dad was thinking out loud. "They must have come on foot and pitched the thing at the window, then run off, maybe down the alley. I can't believe somebody would do this."

Juanita was crying, and Mom took her in her arms. "It's all right, baby. It's all right now."

Abuela Lena stood in the hallway, staring at the mess on the floor. "We must call the police at once. This could have been a tragedy. What if the children had been in the living room? What if somebody had been hit in the head by the cement? Whoever did this is a criminal, a terrible criminal. They must be punished."

"Yes Mama," Ernesto's father said as he dialed 911. Luis Sandoval was a strong man, but his voice shook as he described the incident to the dispatcher. They said a police unit was on the way.

Mom, still holding a softly weeping Juanita in her arms, wondered, "Who would do such a thing? We have no enemies. We've had no trouble with anybody."

Maria Sandoval thought back to the several serious conversations with her mother in Los Angeles, before the family moved back here to the *barrio*. Both Luis and Maria had been born and raised in the *barrio*. Maria's mother was concerned that it was a dangerous place with a lot of gangs and crime. Mrs. Vasquez, Maria's mother, had not wanted the Sandovals to return here. But Ernesto's father had lost his teaching job in Los Angeles during the budget cuts in the district. When he was offered a job at Cesar Chavez High School, they had no choice but to move.

"Dad," Ernesto asked nervously, "I met some real bad-looking dudes on my way home from school . . . guys with shaved heads and tattoos. They wanted to know if

I was your kid. They were ticked off about you going around the neighborhood talking to kids. They figured you might stumble across stuff they want to keep hidden."

"Well, that probably had nothing to do with what happened tonight." Dad dismissed the idea. "Anyway, I'm not going to let some sick punks stop me from trying to get kids off the streets and back in school. I won't be ruled by fear."

"Luis," Mom asserted with a sharpness in her voice that Ernesto rarely heard from his mother. "It's well and good that you want to save kids. But you can't put yourself and your family in danger!"

CHAPTER THREE

As they waited for the police, Ernesto couldn't remember his mother being so angry in a long time. Juanita was in her arms, and even brave little Katalina was wide-eyed with fear. "Luis," Mom commanded, "your first obligation is to your family—the safety of your family!"

Maria Sandoval was shocked by the attack on her home and her family. She was frightened for her husband, her children, *Abuela*. Ernesto didn't blame his mother for feeling as she did. Yet he sympathized deeply with what his father was trying to do. Ernesto now regretted telling his parents what those punks on the street said. He felt he shouldn't have said that they were ticked off at Dad, that they resented his walking the streets and talking to kids. Ernesto realized now that saying those things was like tossing a can of gasoline on a fire. But he had spoken without thinking. At the same time, he wondered whether Dad *wouldn't* be better off just sticking to teaching and giving up on his crusade to rescue the dropouts and the gang wannabes.

"Maria," Dad spoke softly. "I keep remembering my friend Eddie Garcia. He saved my life. I would have drowned that day in the rip tide if Eddie hadn't risked his life to save me. Then Eddie fell in with the gangs. If only there had been an adult, a teacher, a cop, or *somebody* to turn Eddie around . . . I tried, but I was just a kid like him. I didn't know the right moves. He had a good mind. He was a whiz in math. He might have been an engineer, an inventor. Instead he's doing time, rotting in prison. And Rueben . . . if somebody had tried to help Rueben, he might not have OD'd. He wouldn't have died at twenty, before he had begun to live. If somebody had taken the time, the risk . . ."

"Luis, I understand what you're saying," Mom responded in a less angry voice. "But you made somebody out there so mad that they threw a chunk of concrete into a window. Our little girls might've been killed! What will they do next? We're not dealing with bad little boys who put graffiti on fences. We're dealing with hardened criminals who are so anxious to protect their dirty crimes that they're willing to hurt people who look too closely."

"We don't even know for sure that a gangbanger threw that chunk of concrete," Dad protested. "Maybe I gave a bad grade to some kid in class who's got a terrible anger problem that I never noticed. Maybe whoever threw that concrete didn't even know why they did it. A few years ago a kid tossed a big rock over a freeway overpass. It crashed through a sunroof and paralyzed a brilliant young college student for life."

CHAPTER THREE

"Luis, you're grasping at straws," Mom persisted. "It had to be one of those creeps out there on the street. They're only interested in dealing drugs and selling guns. And you made them afraid by shining too bright a light into their dirty little secrets."

Then another thought crossed Ernesto's mind. He remembered the hatred in Clay Aguirre's eyes when he looked at him with Naomi. Could Clay have thrown the concrete? Was he that furious over losing Naomi? Ernesto didn't think Clay would go that far, but who really knew anybody else's mind? How many times after a horrible crime do friends and family insist that the guilty person was not capable of such evil?

The police car pulled into the driveway, and two officers came to the door. One was a woman with close-cropped hair and a grim face. The other officer was younger, in his twenties, almost boyish.

When the officers were inside, Mom described what had happened. "We were just sitting around after our dinner when we heard the glass break, then a thud. There was this mess here in the living room. When we looked outside, there was no sign of a car or anything."

"You didn't touch anything, right?" the female officer asked, as she studied the scene and took some pictures.

"Nothing," Dad replied. He looked so sad, and Ernesto felt sorry for him. No father loved his family more or strove harder to protect them. It was breaking his heart that some good actions of his somehow put him and his family in danger.

Juanita was still whimpering, but Katalina looked angry. "I hope you guys catch those bad guys and put them in jail forever and ever," she fumed.

The older officer almost smiled at the little girl before saying in a terse voice, "We'll do our best."

There was no note on the concrete chunk, which the officers put into a bag. Then they went outside to check for footprints in the front lawn and tire tracks in the driveway. They took pictures. When they came inside again, the younger officer asked, "Do you know of anyone angry enough at you to have done this?"

"I'm a history teacher at Chavez High," Luis Sandoval answered. "I'm not aware of any serious problems with any of the students."

Maria Sandoval spoke up. "My husband is very dedicated. He really cares about the kids, and a lot of them drop out of school before graduation. So he goes around the streets and strikes up conversations with kids who've dropped out, trying to get them back to school. Some gangbangers just told our son that they resent my husband getting too close to their turf. Ernie, tell the officers what you told us."

Dad looked pained, but Ernesto relayed what he was told by the boys with shaved heads.

The woman officer asked, "Do you know the names of these young men?"

"No," Ernesto replied. "I'd never seen them before. But they had shaved heads and lots of tattoos on their arms and shoulders."

"Tattoos of what?" the younger officer asked.

"I don't remember exactly, but one of them had this big vulture on his shoulders. I remember that," Ernesto told him.

The two police officers exchanged a look. The woman said, "Condor." The young male officer nodded.

The officers told the Sandoval family that they would be in touch if they learned anything. In the meantime, they advised that maybe the family should get a security system. Then they left.

"Ernie," Dad suggested in a crestfallen voice, "let's you and me get some plywood from the shed so we can patch that hole in the window. We'll get new glass in as quickly as we can, but tonight it needs to be closed up."

"Sure, Dad," Ernesto responded.

"Maybe we need steel bars for the windows," *Abuela* said. All during the time the police were here, she had said nothing. Now she stood there, arms folded, with a worried look on her face. "I don't say this because I'm afraid for myself, but for the children," she explained. "I am a *mujer anciana,* but they are young."

Maria Sandoval looked at her mother-in-law. "I agree, Mama. That would be a good idea. Many of the houses around here have burglar bars."

"It makes the house look like a prison," Dad remarked in a forlorn voice. "But if that will bring you comfort, we'll ask the landlord."

Ernesto went with his father to get the plywood. As they walked to the shed, Ernesto spoke.

"Dad, I'm sorry I mentioned those gangbangers."

"No, no, Ernie. It's all right," Dad assured him. "You had to. You heard them say that stuff, and it may be relevant. The police needed to know. They seemed to know of a boy with a vulture tattoo. Did you notice the knowing looks they gave each other? They called him 'Condor.' I've heard that name myself. He's a violent drug dealer. He's hardcore. The police haven't been able to bust him yet. If they could, I think the whole *barrio* would be safer."

Back in the living room, Ernesto and his father removed the broken glass and fit the plywood into the window frame. The room turned dark and depressing. When Ernesto went to his room to do his math homework, he heard his parents talking in the living room until very late. They were talking softly, sadly. Eavesdropping in the darkened hall, Ernesto saw that they had come together, sitting on the couch, very close. Dad's arm was around Mom's shoulders.

Back in his bed, Ernesto tried to sleep. But troubled thoughts crashed through his mind. He had not told the police about the one boy in the group of four whose name he did know—Manny Martinez. Ernesto had deliberately neglected to name the boy because he was Naomi's brother. Now

Ernesto felt guilty about not telling the police.

Maybe Manny hurled the concrete chunk. He looked like a weak, easily manip- ulated kid. Maybe the others had given him the job of tossing the concrete into the Sandoval house. They often picked the newbies for some act of criminal violence so they could prove they were worthy to join the gang. Telling the police about Manny could have been a valuable clue.

Ernesto tossed and turned, unable to sleep. He kept trying to convince himself that Manny wasn't out there in the darkness. He hoped Manny wasn't the one who hurled the concrete that could have seriously injured Katalina or Juanita. What if they had been in the wrong place at the wrong time? By Sunday morning, Ernesto was drenched in perspiration.

After school on Monday, Ernesto jogged over to the Martinez house on Bluebird Street. He was using the pretext that Mom was writing a book about a nice pit bull and his friendship with a cat. The dog was based on Brutus, the pit bull the Martinez family owned. Ernesto figured he'd take a couple pictures of Brutus for the illustrator of his mother's book. Then, once he had a pleasant conversation going with Felix Martinez, he could maybe segue into Manny's situation.

Felix Martinez usually spent some time in the afternoon playing with Brutus, tossing him a ball. As Ernesto walked up, he was glad to see the man and the dog in the front yard.

"Hi Mr. Martinez," Ernesto called out.

"Hey Ernie," Mr. Martinez said in a cheerful voice, "How's it goin'?" He seemed in a good mood. He had already had two cans of beer, which put him in a jovial mood. With the third beer, he usually started getting ugly.

"Good!" Ernesto said cheerfully. "Naomi's told you about my mom's book about a nice pit bull, right?"

"Yeah," Mr. Martinez recalled. "She said something about it. She said you guys got the idea from old Brutus here. That's pretty cool. All the idiots out there who think all pit bulls are dangerous, they need to meet Brutus. He's like a poodle! Even my scaredy-cat wife likes him now. She was so afraid of him at first that she locked herself in the kitchen. But now she wants him to sleep in our bedroom!"

With permission, Ernesto snapped a few pictures of Brutus on his phone. Then he figured he'd make his move. "You know, Mr. Martinez, me and Naomi are good friends and I like your son, Zack. But I never got to know your other two sons 'cause we were living in Los Angeles when they moved away."

"You didn't miss nothin', not knowing those lousy bums," Mr. Martinez sneered, his mood turning sour at the mention of his older sons.

"I uh . . . met Manny, your son, the other day when I was walking home from school," Ernesto blurted.

"He ain't my son," the man raged. "He ain't my son no more. Him and his older brother. I washed my hands of them two a long time ago. Trash is what they are. It's her fault, her in there." He nodded toward the house.

"That idiot wife of mine," he began to rant. "She spoiled those boys. When they started goin' bad, they needed the strap. She'd be yammerin' about child abuse and stuff. They didn't get the discipline they needed. So they turned into garbage. Wanna beer?"

Ernesto murmured a "No thanks." And Mr. Martinez reached into a cooler by his lawnchair and fetched a cold can.

"When I was a kid, I was the same way," the man continued. "I sassed my old man, but I done it just once. My old man, he stood me against a tree without no shirt on, and he whipped me bloody. Blood was run-nin' down into my trousers. That made a man of me. I got a job now, I'm the best heavy equipment operator they got down there. I earn good money. Guys respect me. I'm a foreman. I make a good life for us, for that stupid woman in there and Naomi and Zack. I'm a respectable member of the neighborhood. If I'd had my way with Orlando and Manny, they'd be fine now." Mr. Martinez seemed as contemplative as a man like him could get.

"Mr. Martinez," Ernesto began, "Manny looked really down. He's skinny and sick looking and—"

"Yeah, he's probably on drugs," the father nodded. "Cocaine, meth, the whole *enchilada*. I know that. You ain't tellin' me nothin' I don't know. Pretty soon we'll get a call from the cops that he OD'd and he's dead in some alley. She'll expect me to fork over the money for some nice funeral, and I don't even want to do that. I don't need for that Padre Benito down at the church to have some maudlin service for the bum, like he was a decent kid. Let them put him in an unmarked grave for all I care. But her in there, she'll make a fuss. Then I'll end up sittin' there in that church where I don't never go, and listenin' to them singin' about angels and stuff." The man shook his head furiously.

"You don't want to try to contact him or anything, huh?" Ernesto asked.

Mr. Martinez laughed. "Ernie, I don't want to insult you or nothin'. But you're a wimp, like your father. Luis Sandoval was always one of those bleedin' heart wimps who thinks everything can be solved by a little love and kindness. It ain't that way in the real world. Manny's a lost cause. Nothin' anybody can do now. Not now. Not after her in there ruined him with her coddlin'."

Felix Martinez took a step toward Ernesto and unexpectedly put a hand on his shoulder. "Lissen up, boy, because I'm talkin' turkey to you now. You got the hots for my girl, Naomi. And you ain't been able to figure out why she don't feel the same way about you. Lemme tell you. Lemme clue you in. Clay Aguirre, he's macho. He's a real guy. Chicks like that. They like a masculine guy who isn't afraid to be a little rough and tough. Y'hear what I'm sayin'? You gotta get a little backbone, Ernie. If you show Naomi you're a real guy, not a wimp, you just might get lucky. And listen, I wouldn't mind if you and Naomi clicked. You're a weakling, Sandoval, but you're a darn good kid. Luis Sandoval's done all right by Maria. And I know you'd take good care of Naomi. But first you gotta toughen up, *muchacho*."

Ernesto looked at the man with disgust. Felix Martinez had seen his own daughter with a black eye. He had to know what Clay Aguirre did. Yet he admired the boy and wanted Ernesto to be more like him.

"Mr. Martinez," Ernesto replied coldly, "I don't think Naomi wanted to be punched in the face by Clay Aguirre like she was. I don't think any girl or woman wants that."

A strange looked came over the man's face. "Sometimes," he spoke slowly, "a man has to show his woman who's boss. Sometimes, if the woman is lucky, her man doesn't have to do that too many times until she gets the message."

Ernesto's disgust deepened. Zack came out then, and Ernesto used that as an excuse to leave. "Hey Zack!" Ernesto hailed, returning to the sidewalk and jogging away.

Zack, Brutus, and Mr. Martinez, with his cooler in tow, all went into the house.

In the distance, Ernesto spotted Naomi coming in the opposite direction, riding her bike home. She'd stayed late at school to help Yvette Ozono sign up for the girls soccer team. Yvette really wanted to play soccer. Her friends thought that was just the thing to get her more involved at Cesar Chavez High School.

Ernesto lingered a few moments until Naomi arrived. She smiled at Ernesto and asked, "What're you doing here, Ernie?"

Ernesto held up his phone. "I needed some pictures of Brutus. Mom's book illustrator is working on the dog in the story and, after all, Brutus was the inspiration."

"That's cute," Naomi said.

"You know, Naomi," Ernesto told her, "a really horrible thing happened at our house last night. Somebody threw a big chunk of concrete through out picture window."

"Oh my God!" Naomi gasped. "Oh Ernie, nobody got hurt, did they?"

"Thankfully no," Ernesto answered. "We'd just finished eating in the dining room. No one was in the living room. We heard the crash, and the whole window was splintered all over the floor."

"You called the police, didn't you?" Naomi asked.

"Yeah, they came and took evidence," Ernesto replied.

"Oh Ernie, who would do such an awful thing?" Naomi cried.

"I don't know," Ernesto shook his head, befuddled. "My dad has been spending a lot of time walking around talking to kids who've dropped out of school, trying to get them back on track. This one dude told me some of the homeboys are ticked off at him.

They think he's gonna stumble on their rotten deals and bring the law down on them. Maybe what happened last night had to do with that."

"I'm so sorry, Ernie," Naomi sympathized. "Your dad is such a great guy. I don't know another teacher at our school who cares so much for the kids. It's so fabulous that he brought guys like Dom and Carlos back to school. They were about ready to ditch school, and now they're really excited about it. And look what he did for Yvette. You can't believe how bright she is. She's even into math! If your dad hadn't taken an interest in her, she'd just be lost." Naomi seemed near tears. "Oh Ernie, I feel so sad for your family and for you."

"Mom is really scared," Ernesto remarked. "She wants to put up burglar bars and stuff." Ernesto wondered whether he should tell Naomi now about her brother being with those guys who warned Ernesto about his father. Ernesto thought for a moment. Then he said, "Naomi, your brother,

Manny, he's out there on the streets, you know, with those gangbangers."

Naomi hung her head. "I know. I haven't talked to him in years. My father said I couldn't. I think by now Manny has forgotten all of us. Mom hasn't heard from him, and neither have I. He's two years older than me, two and a half. He's about nineteen. Manny got kicked out of the house when he was sixteen. I was almost fourteen. I remember crying and crying."

Naomi was silent for a while and then spoke again. "You know what, Ernie? My older brothers, Orlando and Manny, they had this little garage band. They let me sing sometimes. We had make-believe gigs in other kids' houses. Manny wasn't bad to me at all. He was a good brother. Orlando too. I miss them, Ernie. But by now, Manny probably doesn't even know who I am. If he saw me on the street, he wouldn't recognize me."

"Naomi," Ernesto admitted, "I talked a little bit to Manny. He's hanging with real bad dudes, but I don't think he's one of them yet. He said he'd seen you and me walking together from school. He wanted to know if you were my girlfriend. Manny looks bad, skinny and shaky, like he's doing pills. But, Naomi, he asked me to say 'Hi' to you."

"Did he really say that?" Naomi asked, her beautiful violet eyes widening.

"Yeah, he did," Ernesto affirmed. "He hasn't forgotten you."

"I wish . . . I wish there was something I could do to help him," Naomi said wistfully. "But if he came near the house, my dad would call the police. Mom is really hurting because she doesn't have any contact with Manny or Orlando. Her heart is breaking."

"Naomi," Ernesto objected, "it doesn't seem fair that your father forbids a mother to see her own boys. I mean, I know he's your father and you respect him, Naomi. But it's just not fair."

"About three years ago," Naomi explained, "they had this really horrible fight, my father and Orlando. I wasn't even home. I was glad for that. I was staying with a girlfriend. Dad and Orlando started fighting, and Orlando hit Dad. He knocked him down. I mean, that was so awful. I love both my brothers, even now, but Orlando had no right to hit his father. Can you imagine hitting your own father? Dad threw all his stuff out into the front yard. He changed the locks on the doors. He told Orlando he can't ever come back to the house because of what he did. And Mom and I, we haven't seen him in three years."

"It must be hard on your mom," Ernesto commented.

Naomi nodded. She seemed about to say more, but her father came outside again. He'd drunk his third or fourth can of beer. "You comin' in to dinner, Naomi?" he hollered. "Your mother has put the slop on the table. It's even worse when it's cold."

"See you, Ernie," Naomi said quickly, turning and hurrying in the house.

CHAPTER FOUR

Ernesto jogged to the pizzeria to do his shift. The *barrio* looked so peaceful this time of day, at dusk. Kids were riding their skateboards, twisting and turning, and coming down with amazing agility. The skateboards clattered, and the kids screamed with laughter. Guys were mowing their lawns, and you could begin to smell the aromas of cooking dinners. Ernesto looked at the skateboarders— boys, eleven or twelve, maybe a little older. They were just kids. They loved baseball and football. Some of them were already into rock and rap. They formed innocent little gangs that were about fun and games.

But in a few years some of them would turn into guys like Condor and Coyote. The street was like a nightmare scenario, an evil spell cast over the young. It was like a deadly disease that struck boys of a certain age, sending them to prison or an early grave. On some of their grave markers, bewildered parents would call them "good," "precious," "sweet." They would never quite understand what had happened to their children.

Ernesto knew that the key to avoiding prison and death was education. His father knew it too. Ernesto knew a lot of guys at Cesar Chavez High School who could someday be gangbangers. They saw bad dudes with flashy cars and thick wads of money, and they wanted that kind of life—easy money. The gangbangers were dropouts, and dropouts were heroes. Ernesto's father was trying to push education on the students whether they wanted it or not.

Luis Sandoval cared about the kids, especially the losers. His face lit up at the thought that he had kept Dom Reynosa and Carlos

Negrete in school. That he'd brought Yvette back to school. Now they'd graduate. Some of them might go to college. The street could- n't claim them anymore. They had soared above the dirty business that tried to suck out their hearts and souls before they could even become men and women.

That was why Luis Sandoval walked the streets of the *barrio,* looking for kids to rescue. He was a shepherd looking for lost sheep who could be led back to the fold before it was too late for them. And Ernesto now felt that a stinking chunk of concrete hurled through the window by a punk threat- ened to put an end to all that good work.

With a heavy heart, Ernesto went into the pizza shop to start work.

After school the next day, Ernesto and the other boys from Chavez's track team gath- ered on the field. Coach Muñoz was going to make the decision on who would try out for which race and who would run in the relay. He would pick the fastest boy to anchor the relay team. Chavez was playing Wilson, and they had never beaten Wilson—or any other school. Gus Muñoz was in the twilight of his career, and the last time his track team had won anything was twelve years ago.

Julio Avila was primed for the tryouts. Even Jorge Aguilar and Eddie Gonzales looked pumped. Ernesto had been running relentlessly, and he was determined to be the anchor in the relay, running that all important last lap.

Julio Avila's father watched from the sidelines, as he usually did. He was a down-on-his-luck guy with only one claim to fame: his vibrant, amazingly athletic son. Julio wanted desperately to please his father. Julio had just one living parent, the grimy old man with the threadbare suit and sadness in his eyes. Julio was the only good thing that had ever happened to the old man, and the son was determined to make his father proud.

After all the boys had run their best, Coach Muñoz decided that both Ernesto and Julio would run in the hundred-yard dash. For the relay, Coach Muñoz announced, "We have two guys who are really good, but I'm going with Julio in the anchor spot."

So Julio would get to run the last lap, leading the Cougars to victory. Ernesto wanted to run the last lap so badly he could taste it. But today Julio was the fastest on the team, and it was only right that he got the anchor spot. Seeing that old man out there in the stands jumping up and down for joy, Ernesto figured, would take some of the sting out of his disappointment.

Julio was grinning from ear to ear as he high-fived his father. Ernesto walked over to the Avilas and he said, "Okay, Julio, you took it away from me, but listen up. I'm gonna run the most amazing first lap you ever saw. By the time the third guy hands you the baton for the last lap, you won't have much to do, 'cause the relay'll be a cinch."

Julio grinned. "Go for it, Ernie," he urged.

Ernesto put out his hand and Julio took it. Mr. Avila looked at his son and then at Ernesto. "This is your friend, eh, Julio?" he asked.

"Yeah Dad, " Julio said, "*mi amigo*."

"Hey Julio," Ernesto suggested, "since you got the anchor, we need to go over to Hortencia's and celebrate. Come on, Mr. Avila, Julio." Ernesto saw Naomi then, and he shouted to her. "Hey Naomi, we're going over to Hortencia's for tamales. Come on." Naomi had come to watch the tryouts, and Ernesto wondered whether she'd come to watch him. He didn't have any illusions about her being even close to dating him. But maybe she at least cared enough to watch him run.

Naomi came walking over, a smile on her face. "You guys were both awesome," she complimented them. "I think for the first time ever, we're gonna whip Wilson. Those Wolverines won't have so much to howl about for a change. Coach Muñoz'll be retiring soon, and it'd be so cool to send him off a winner."

They all crossed the street to Hortencia's and took a booth. Hortencia seemed especially radiant these days, and Ernesto couldn't help attributing her happiness to Oscar Perez. Dating a guy like that had to be exciting for her.

"You guys," Hortencia announced, "Oscar is gonna come here with his trio on Sunday night. I'm opening the patio 'cause there'll be tons of people. You gotta come."

"Sure," Ernesto agreed. "I'll be here. I've never seen his trio."

"Me too," Naomi chimed in, looking at Ernesto. "If there's room for me in the Volvo."

Ernesto's heart skipped a beat. "I think there'll be room, Naomi," he said, not wanting to show his excitement too much.

All the way home, Ernesto kept telling himself this would not be a date with Naomi. This would just be giving a friend a ride to the concert at Hortencia's.

When Ernesto got home, Katalina was playing in the front yard. She demanded, "Did you get the anchor in the relay race, Ernie?"

"No, but I get to run a lap, and I'll show 'em," Ernesto replied cheerfully.

"No fair!" Katalina said grumpily. "You shoulda got it."

"It's okay, Kat," he consoled her.

He was glad to see the men working on installing the new picture window. It was double-paned and much more resistant to damage.

"It's beautiful," Mom declared, "and it'll make the room warmer in winter and cooler in summer. And now we have a security system too. Did you see the sign out front? Anybody walks onto our property'll trip a sensor." Mom seemed happy and relieved after the scare they had.

On Sunday evening, Ernesto went to Naomi's house to pick her up. The weather was clear and beautiful. Santa Ana winds

had been blowing earlier in the day. Everything was sharp and vivid, including the
moon and the stars.

"I wonder what Oscar's trio is like,"
Naomi wondered, as they headed for the
tamale shop. "He's so good, but the trio has
got to make the music even more exciting."

Quite a few cars were already parked
at Hortencia's when they arrived. Ernesto's
heart sank when he saw Clay Aguirre's
Mustang. But then he noticed Clay had a
pretty girl with him, Mira Nuñez, also a
junior. Ernesto hoped that was a sign that
Clay had given up on getting Naomi back.
Maybe he was hooking up with somebody
else. Ernesto did feel a little sorry for Mira
Nuñez, though.

The minute Ernesto and Naomi walked
into the patio, Clay turned sharply and
stared at them, ignoring Mira completely.
That made Ernesto sick.

Naomi tried to act unconcerned. She
focused on Oscar Perez as the handsome
young man adjusted his equipment on the

stage. The three men in the trio appeared. All seemed much younger than the thirty-something Perez, but all three were strikingly good-looking. They had thick, longish black hair, and they wore crisp white shirts and dark jeans.

"Ernie!" Naomi cried out with such intensity that Ernesto's blood ran cold. He thought she'd been hurt or something.

"*What? What's the matter?*" he demanded, turning toward her.

"That's my brother!" Naomi gasped. "That's Orlando! The one on the left! Oh Ernie!" Naomi was clutching Ernesto's arm so tightly that her fingers were hurting him.

Ernesto looked up at the boy on the left. He could see Felix Martinez in the deep, dark, almost fierce eyes, the determined set to his mouth, the dark skin. Felix was much darker than his wife, just as Luis Sandoval was darker than Ernesto's mother. But when the music started, the boy's expression turned joyful, and a brilliant smile broke his dark face.

Tears streamed down Naomi's face. Ernesto put his arms around her and pulled her gently and protectively against him. He didn't care what Clay Aguirre might be thinking. "Ohhh Ernie," Naomi whispered in a shaky voice. "I haven't seen my brother in three years! He looks wonderful!"

Oscar Perez and his trio sang Mexican folk songs and popular American songs. To the delight of the young audience, they even did some rap. Ernesto noticed that Naomi didn't take her eyes off her brother. In the middle of one of his solos, Orlando looked right at his sister and smiled. During the intermission, Orlando came over to where Naomi was sitting with her friends, and he reached out his arms. Naomi fled into them.

"*Mi hermana!*" Orlando said in an emotional voice, holding her at a distance from himself. "When I last saw you, you were a little girl. Now you are a beautiful woman!"

"Oh Orlando, I miss you so much," Naomi told him. "Mama misses you. Every

night she says a rosary for you and for
Manny. I hear her in her room praying with
the candles lit in the glass with Our Lady of
Guadalupe on it."

"How is Mama?" Orlando asked.

"She is . . . all right, Orlando," Naomi
replied.

"And Manny, do you see him?"
Orlando asked.

"No," Naomi answered.

"But he is okay, huh?" Orlando said.

Ernesto spoke up. "No, he's not."

Orlando looked from his sister to
Ernesto. "Who is this boy, Naomi?" he
asked.

"Ernesto Sandoval, Orlando." Naomi
made the introduction. "He's a special
friend of mine. His father teaches history at
Chavez High. I have him. He's a wonderful
teacher."

Orlando looked right at Ernesto.
Something about his almost sinister stare
reminded Ernesto of Felix Martinez. He
was his father's son in the anger that leaped

quickly to his eyes. Ernesto could easily imagine why the two had clashed so bitterly.

"Why do you say my brother is not okay?" Orlando demanded. "Tell me what you know about him. I am very concerned. In the beginning we texted and talked, but then he had no phone. He vanished."

"He hangs out on the street with gang-bangers, real hardcore guys," Ernesto explained. "I don't think he's one yet. He's probably a gofer for them. But he looks bad. He looks like he doesn't get enough to eat, and he's dirty like he's homeless."

Orlando clamped his hand to his head and cursed. Then he asked, "After the classes are over tomorrow at your school, Ernesto, will you help me to find my brother? I must find him."

"Yeah, sure," Ernesto agreed. "Come to the school parking lot. You and Naomi can ride in my Volvo. I'm pretty sure I can find him. The gangbangers and the wannabes have their regular hangouts." Then Ernesto remembered.

"I have to be at work by four," he told Orlando. "Should I call and say I might be late?"

"Nah man," Orlando replied, "you don't have to do that for me. If it takes too long, we'll try again. OK?"

"Cool," Ernesto agreed. "But let's hope we have enough time. I think I know where to look."

After school the next day, Orlando was already waiting by the Volvo when Ernesto and Naomi walked up to it. They left the school, heading for the deli and the around-the-clock convenience store where guys were always hanging. They circled the block without seeing anybody. Then Ernesto spotted a gaunt figure checking out the dumpster in the back of the market.

"There he is," Ernesto pointed. They'd found him right away.

"Pull over!" Orlando commanded. When Ernesto did, Orlando leaped from the car and sprinted toward his brother. Ernesto and Naomi followed.

Manny turned. He didn't immediately recognize the big guy running toward him as his brother. Orlando had been a skinny kid the last time Manny saw him. The dude coming at him fast looked as though he weighed at least a hundred and seventy. Orlando had short hair before, and now it was long. Manny took off running.

"Manuel!" Orlando shouted as his younger brother fled. The younger boy continued running, but Orlando overtook him, grabbing his shoulders and turning him around. "Manny, it's me! It's Orlando."

Manny looked shocked and a little frightened. He saw Naomi then, and the sight of her calmed him down. Naomi rushed to her brother and hugged him, ignoring how he looked and smelled. She was crying when they separated.

"Whatcha been doin', man?" Orlando demanded, yelling in his brother's face.

"You had my cell number. You coulda called. How come you cut me off?"

Ernesto could see more and more of Felix Martinez in this angry young man. He was tough, almost brutal.

"You been hangin' with creeps, homie. What's *wrong* with you?" Orlando seemed as short on compassion as Felix Martinez. Then he grabbed his younger brother and hugged him. "Man, you could die out here. You're like a skeleton, dude. You look *sick*. Come on, we're goin' to see somebody."

"Who?" Manny gasped. "You ain't takin' me home are you? The old man'll kill me."

Finally Orlando laughed. It wasn't a happy laugh. It was an angry, sneering laugh. "Man, he'd try to kill me too," Orlando declared. "We're gonna see the old man at the church. Padre Benito."

Our Lady of Guadalupe Church was just a block away, a rather shabby-looking little frame building set close to the street. The pastor was Padre Benito, a man about fifty who looked older. When the four of them went into the tiny office, the old priest was sitting there. He wore a white shirt and shiny slacks that had seen better days. The people who attended Sunday Mass at this church did not put much into the collection plate.

"Well, I know you, Ernesto," the priest said. "And Naomi, you come with your mama sometimes, but I don't remember these other two."

"I'm Orlando Martinez," the brother replied, "and this is my brother, Manuel. Our parents, Felix and Linda, they belong to this church. I know my father doesn't show up often, but my mother does."

"Ahhh," the priest sighed. "You used to serve the 7:30 mass. And Manuel, you served at 10:30. Such a long time ago."

Manny said nothing. He hung his head. He hadn't had a bath in a long time. He was shaggy and dirty, but he hadn't cared until now. Now he felt ashamed.

"Padre," Orlando continued, "he's homeless. Our father threw us both out. I've made a good life in Los Angeles. I'm with the Oscar Perez trio. I can't take Manny in now, but I will later. My brother needs a place to clean up, three squares a day until I can arrange something. He's been hanging with the homeboys. I'm afraid pretty soon he'll be in trouble. Can you find him a place where he can hang until I figure something out? I can't just leave him on the street."

The old priest nodded. "I'll call Father Joe. He's is a good man to call when you're in a tight spot."

Padre Benito got on the phone and chatted with somebody for a few minutes. He said there was a sale on potatoes and his car was loaded with a dozen bags. A nice lady at church had donated them for Father Joe. Then he talked about the boy who needed a place. He nodded and put down the phone.

"Manny," Padre said quietly, "I'm going down now with the potatoes. You can ride along."

Orlando Martinez threw an arm around his brother's thin shoulders and told him softly, "Gonna be okay, *mi hermano*."

Manny left for a place called "Father Joe's Village," where they fed thousands of the homeless. They took in teenagers and provided an education. They offered medical and dental care. There was little they didn't do for the desperate, the poor, the abused. Orlando breathed a sigh of relief that Manny would be okay until he came for him.

CHAPTER FIVE

Ernesto and Naomi delivered Orlando to
the bus that would take Oscar Perez and
the rest of the band back to Los Angeles.
They had a gig tomorrow night in Canoga
Park.

They'd found Manny and gotten him to
a safe place in only twenty-five minutes.
They all decided to celebrate with a frozen
yogurt. Seated at a booth at the yogurt shop,
their mood was joyous.

"You have no idea how much Mama
misses you, Orlando," Naomi remarked
over her frozen strawberry yogurt. "I remember being thirteen and coming home
from my girlfriend's house. *You were gone*.
I don't even know exactly why."

"Mama never told you the details?" Orlando asked. Then he shrugged. "Why does that not surprise me?"

"She said you and Dad had an argument and you hit him," Naomi explained.

"Yeah," Orlando acknowledged. "And Mama chose the old *diablo* over me. That's what she did. He was on her case that night. I'd just come home from school, and he was drinking as usual. He slapped her— slapped her hard—and she fell backwards into the sofa. It was too much for me."

"Dad slapped Mama?" Naomi asked. "I never saw that . . ."

"You see what you want to see, *mi hermana*," he chided her. "They call it denial. Anyway, I went after him. He was dumbfounded. He said he would teach me to respect my father . . . *mi padre!* What a sick joke that I would learn respect from him. I punched him good. Yeah, I did. He hit the floor. He ordered me from the house then. He said if I came back, he'd call the cops."

Orlando reflected for a moment. "Mom, she sat there cryin'. She's good at that. She's had a lot of practice. I had fifty dollars in my pocket and two more weeks of high school. I had no job, nothing. I hung out with a cousin 'till I graduated. Mama and the old man, they didn't even come to the graduation. You know what Mama did when he threw me and all my stuff out? *Nada*. That's what she did. She chose him over me."

"Orlando, I was thirteen and Zack was fourteen," Naomi protested. "What was she going to do? Manny was sixteen. Mama never had a job. She never paid a bill. He does everything. He's always provided for us. What was she going to do?"

"We could have all gone to a shelter," Orlando insisted. "She could have divorced him and made him pay support. It's not right to live like that, Naomi. It's not right for a man to put down and ridicule and abuse a woman like that, year after year. It made me sick to my stomach how he would give her digs every day. She didn't clean the house good enough. She was a lousy cook. She was a fool."

Orlando was working up a rage. "He beat her down with his words until she became smaller and smaller, and weaker and weaker. Finally, I guess she just believed all the bad things he said about her. Dad, he's a big talker, talks all the time about what he's interested in. Mama would say a few words. And he'd yell at her, 'Don't you *ever* shut up, woman?' I could see Mama fading before my eyes. And that made me so angry I had begun to hate this man who was my father."

There were tears in Naomi's eyes. "I know Dad is mean to Mom a lot . . . but . . . but she *loves* him. And in his way he loves her . . ."

"*Love?*" Orlando almost screamed. "Such love is a sickness!" He leaned forward, looking right at his sister, with something almost menacing in his eyes. "Naomi, this boy here, Ernesto Sandoval, is he your boyfriend?" he asked.

CHAPTER FIVE

Naomi glanced at Ernesto and answered, "He's a dear friend."

"Listen to me, *muchacha*," Orlando commanded. "If this is not your boyfriend, you find one like him. You keep looking until you find such a boy. If I ever find out you are with a boy who is like our father, I will come and drag you from him. And if I ever hear a boy has treated you like the old *diablo* has treated our mama, I will destroy him!"

Ernesto concentrated on his frozen chocolate yogurt. He could see that Naomi was deeply shaken, but she said nothing.

Later, right before Orlando got out of the Volvo for the bus, Naomi asked him, "Would it be okay if I told Mama about meeting you and Manny, Orlando?"

"Sure," Orlando agreed. "You tell her that I love her. She is always in my heart. She is *mi madre*. Sometime maybe I can see her. But not in *his* house." Orlando reached in his pocket for a card. It bore his name and cell phone number. "Tell Mama to call me.

If we can arrange to meet somewhere later on, I'll buy a nice dinner for everybody. I'll give my mama all the hugs we have missed out on." He had smiled a little before, but now he grinned widely, "It would make me happy for us to be together."

Then, as suddenly as the warm smile came, it vanished into a bitter frown. "But she won't call me. She'd be afraid if he knew he would be angry. She will not call and agree to meet. She cannot do anything for someone he disapproves of. This is how she lives her life. No human being should live their life cowering in fear of someone else. But this is how she does."

The yogurts were finished, and so was the conversation.

"Hey man," Ernesto said, "I gotta get to work."

Ernesto dropped Orlando off at the school lot. When Naomi and Ernesto were alone in the car going home, Naomi sighed. "It was so wonderful to see my brothers, but I feel so sad and strange. I'm glad somebody is going to help Manny. That's a good thing."

"Naomi, are you going to tell your mom about today?" Ernesto asked.

"Yes," Naomi stated. "I'm going to ask her to call Orlando. I know how much it would mean to her to see her boys. She mourns them as if they were dead. Orlando went hard on Mama tonight. He doesn't understand."

"Do you think your father would ever forgive Orlando for what happened?" Ernesto asked.

"Maybe," Naomi guessed, "if Orlando asked for forgiveness. In my father's world, a son must never strike his father."

"I don't think Orlando has it in him to ask for forgiveness for defending his mother," Ernesto commented. "I don't think a man should have to ask forgiveness for doing the right thing."

Naomi said nothing for a moment and then spoke. "Ernie, you don't understand. Your family is so different. Your father is a

very special man. You're lucky, Ernie.
Most of us don't get fathers like Luis
Sandoval. When he stands before the class
in history, I just admire him so much. He's
such a good man, so dedicated. He is well
educated and soft-spoken. Having a father
like that makes it hard for you to understand other men, Ernie."

She seemed close to tears again. "There
are not so many men in this world like Luis
Sandoval. My dad isn't perfect. I know
that. I don't like the way he talks to Mom,
but he does love her. Two years ago, Mama
had serious surgery, and she was in the
hospital for five days. He stayed there the
whole time. For hours he sat at her bedside.
I saw him weeping. He loves her. He cares
for her. I know he's unkind sometimes, and
I hate that, but he buys her nice stuff. If she
sees some new gadget on TV, it's in the
house by the weekend. Dad loves her, and
he loves me and Zack. He even loves
Orlando and Manny. But he's so embittered
by what happened that he hides his

feelings. He's a difficult man, Ernie, but he's always taken care of us. And he's never been unfaithful to my mother. He's my father and . . . *I love him*."

"I know you love your father, Naomi. That's only natural," Ernesto said gently.

"Sometimes good people do bad things, Ernie," Naomi continued, "but that doesn't mean that deep down they aren't good. When I was little, my father would take me to the park to go on the slides and swings. I remember one time there was a cold rain, and I didn't have a heavy coat. So he took off his and gave it to me. He caught a nasty cold, but he said that was okay because it was better than me getting sick."

Ernesto wasn't exactly sure whom Naomi was talking about, her father or Clay Aguirre. Was she trying to justify her father's bad behavior? Was she trying to rationalize getting back with Clay Aguirre? Like her father, Clay too had deeply buried good qualities that were worth looking for.

When Ernesto dropped off Naomi, they exchanged only simple good-byes.

He was a few minutes late for work. But he apologized to his boss and got right to work.

At school on Tuesday, Ernesto noticed that Yvette Ozono was wearing a beautiful lilac-colored pullover, similar to the sweaters Naomi wore. Usually Yvette showed up at school in out-of-date, often threadbare clothing. Her mother was struggling to provide for three children on minimum-wage jobs cleaning office buildings. There was no money for nice clothing for the children. Yvette was very slim, about Naomi's size, and Ernesto suspected that maybe Naomi had given her some of her pullovers. Naomi would do something like that. She would convince Yvette that she was overwearing a certain sweater and was about to donate it to the thrift store unless Yvette wanted it. The truth was that Naomi was always at the mall getting the latest fashions.

"Hey Yvette," Ernesto commented. "You look great in that color."

Yvette smiled. She was a really beautiful girl, but most of the time in the past she looked drab and sad. Now her new sweater matched the light in her eyes. "Oh, thanks, Ernie. I love this pullover," she responded. "I could never buy one like this, but Naomi was cleaning out her closet. She said she was bored with some of her stuff, and did I want something? Isn't that cool?"

"It fits you great," Ernesto said.

"Yeah, and I got two others," Yvette beamed. "Naomi is the nicest girl I ever met. I'm so lucky to have a friend like her."

"She *is* nice," Ernesto agreed. Naomi was as kindhearted as she was beautiful. That's what made her so appealing to Ernesto. Most girls with her figure and her looks would be stuck-up. But she lived her life as if she didn't know how lovely she really was. That's why Ernesto was willing to risk Clay Aguirre's wrath to get close to her, why he was willing to be patient.

"You know Ernie," Yvette went on, "if she's not pushing Tessie in her wheelchair, she's making sure there's enough food in the homeless shelter Chavez High is supporting. I love it here at Chavez, Ernie. I'm so happy your dad came to my place and nagged me to come back to school. After I dropped out, I was just stuck in that bad neighborhood with a bunch of losers."

Just then Dom Reynosa came along. He looked at Yvette and grinned. "Hey, get movin', girl. We're gonna be late for Cabral's class if we don't hurry. You know what he does to kids who come in late. He makes them sit in that tiny chair up front that he got from a day care center!"

Ernesto blinked. José Cabral was one of the new young teachers hired at Cesar Chavez High. He was a graduate of the Massachusetts Institute of Technology. A local boy, he returned to the *barrio* after his excellent education to pass it along to other kids. Ernesto didn't have him, but the word around school was that he was electrifying.

"You in Cabral's class, Yvette?" Ernesto asked in surprise.

Yvette giggled. Ernesto had never heard her giggle before. "Yeah, and Mr. Cabral put me and Dom in the geek squad. He said we were two of his top students."

"Wow Yvette!" Ernesto cried. "And Dom too? That's really awesome. I wish I was that good in math."

Dom shrugged, "I always liked math. The other classes bore me. But now I understand I gotta put up with stupid English stories and stuff about the ancient Romans, just so I can get my math in. This guy, Cabral, he does all kinds of neat stuff in class. It's like going to a sci-fi movie sometimes."

As they walked along, Yvette spoke. "My mom never thought I was smart. I got good grades in math in school. But she always said I'd slip when I got into really hard stuff like algebra and trig. To me, though, it seems to get easier, not harder. Mr. Cabral has a poster in his classroom. It has a picture of that famous Bolivian teacher, Jaime Escalante. It says, 'Calculus need not be made easy. It is easy already.'"

Dom and Yvette headed into Mr. Cabral's room. Ernesto noticed Dom slipping an arm around the girl's shoulders, and Ernesto smiled. Ernesto thought to himself that neither kid, Dom nor Yvette, would be in that classroom—and doing great work—if it were not for Luis Sandoval. Ernesto was so proud of his father.

At the end of the school day, Ernesto worked up enough courage to ask Naomi to come to Sunday dinner at his house. It wouldn't be like a real date, but it might just lead to a real date. It would be just a friend asking another friend over to dinner.

"My grandmother, *Abuela* Lena," Ernesto began, "she loves cooking, and she pushes Mom out of the kitchen half the time. When *Abuela* moved in with us, we thought she was going to be sitting around not doing much, but she's come to life. Over at *Tía* Magda's house she spent most of the time watching TV. I guess they discouraged her from doing stuff, but Mom lets her shine. Well, anyway, she's making one of her specialties on Sunday, and she asked me if you could come, Naomi. I've told her a lot about you and she'd like to meet you."

Naomi smiled. "Well, I sure wouldn't want to disappoint your grandmother!"

"Then you can come? We have dinner around one," Ernesto said.

"Okay," Naomi promised. "Bluebird Street is just a block from Wren, so I'll come strolling over, Ernie."

Ernesto was feeling optimistic again. He was making a little progress. He made up his mind that he wouldn't bring up anything unpleasant at the dinner table. No problems. Nothing about Orlando or Manny. It would just be a happy family dinner, with *Abuela* having a chance to show off her cooking skills. For many years she cooked for her husband and their five children. Lena Sandoval was the best cook in the *barrio;* that was common knowledge.

Hortencia gained her marvelous tamale-making skills at her mother's side.

Late that Sunday morning, *Abuela* was busy in the kitchen. She had done much of the work the night before, putting pineapple juice, lime juice, white vinegar, cloves, dried oregano, ground pepper, minced chili pepper, and vegetable oil in a Ziploc bag. She added chicken pieces, put the concoction in the refrigerator, and marinated it all night. Now *Abuela* was grilling the chicken, and heavenly aromas filled the Sandoval house and floated down the street.

"Mama," Ernesto's mother noted, "that smells so good!" She glanced at Ernesto, "Naomi will love it."

Naomi came walking over at quarter to one, and everybody gathered in the dining room. As she always did, *Abuela* led the blessing.

"Oooooo," Juanita cried, "I'm so glad you came to live with us, *Abuela!*" She had "pretasted" the chicken.

Ernesto's mother laughed. "So much for *my* cooking, but never mind. I write books about pit bulls!"

"You're a wonderful cook, Maria," *Abuela* stated loyally. She liked all the spouses of her children, but she had a special affection for Maria Sandoval. Ernesto often thought his dad's mom loved his mother more than mom's mom loved his dad.

"Yes Maria," Dad concurred, "you are a splendid cook."

It was not lost on Naomi how everybody came together to make Maria Sandoval feel special. Nobody wanted her to feel slighted. Ernesto noted a faint sadness in Naomi's eyes. Her father always criticized his wife's cooking, and Zack just laughed. Naomi felt guilty about keeping quiet when Dad was unkind. Naomi thought her own mother was a very good cook but received scant credit.

"Dad," Ernesto announced, "I caught something at school the other day that just blew my mind. Maybe you already know it, but I was amazed. Yvette Ozono and Dom

Reynosa are in Mr. Cabral's math class, and they're doing great. They're in the geek squad as top students."

Dad grinned. "Isn't that something?" he beamed.

"Dad," Ernesto went on, "neither one of them would be in school if you hadn't reached out to them."

"Well," Dad demurred, "if there's something I can do to help kids along, I should. These kids who're good in math, they're the hope of America's technical future."

Then he switched the focus off himself. "José Cabral is just in his twenties, you know, and what a cool, bright guy. He gets this scholarship to go to MIT and graduates with honors, turns down excellent job offers on the East Coast, and comes back here to help the kids in the neighborhood where he grew up. Really an inspiring guy."

Mom looked up then, pensive for a moment. Then she said, "I met his wife at our last faculty wives get-together. She's some kind of genius too. She has a master's degree, and she's working for a high-tech company developing new gizmos I don't even understand. We got to talking, you know. I mentioned to her how that chunk of concrete came through our living room window the other night and I was scared stiff. I was almost ready to get out of town . . ."

Ernesto was looking at his mother and listening intently. Dad was too.

"I asked her—Jennifer's her name—if she was afraid of living around here with the gangs and all. I mean, her husband married her in Massachusetts, and they both could have stayed there getting good jobs. But she said it was her husband's dream to come home and make a difference here. I asked her if her husband was afraid to ask her to make such a sacrifice. She said the sweetest thing. She said, 'Jose and I love each other. I want his dreams to come true as much as he does. If his life is here, then my life is here. *With love there is no fear.*'"

CHAPTER SIX

After Sunday dinner, Ernesto and Naomi walked back to her house. "Your grandmother is a wonderful cook and a doll," Naomi remarked. "I really enjoyed that dinner. Thanks for inviting me, Ernie."

"Anytime," Ernesto said. He wanted to reach out and put his arm around her lovely, soft shoulders, as Dom did with Yvette. He wanted to touch her velvet skin and feel his fingertips tingle. But he didn't dare. Not yet. She always described him as a good friend, never using the term he longed to hear: "boyfriend."

"Naomi, did you tell your mom about meeting your brothers?" Ernesto asked.

"Yeah, I did," she replied. "She started crying like crazy. She wanted to know how they were doing, are they okay, all that. I told her Orlando is doing great. Manny, not so much. But Manny is gonna be okay. I told her that. I told her that Orlando wants to meet us, including Manny, and go to dinner but that he said she wouldn't go for that because of Dad."

Ernesto turned toward the girl. They stopped walking. "And?" Ernesto pressed.

"She's really nervous about it, Ernie, but she wants to do it. She wants to see her boys with all her heart. Oh Ernie, you've done so many favors for me that I hate to ask you for another big one. But I told Mom I'd ask you. If you would drive me and Mom to a restaurant, we could meet my brothers there. Dad wouldn't have to know anything about it. Mom goes to visit her sister sometimes, and she's gone for several hours. Dad doesn't complain about that. She could say she's going to see her sister, I'm going too, and you're driving us."

Naomi's beautiful eyes fixed on Ernesto's face. They were the most beautiful eyes he had ever seen. They made him weak in the knees. He wanted to grab her, kiss her, not let go.

"Sure Naomi," Ernesto agreed, "I'll do that for you and your mom."

"Oh Ernie," Naomi cried, standing there, face to face with him. In all the time they had been friends, Naomi had never kissed Ernesto. He fantasized about it, yearned for it, dreamed of it. But it never happened—until then. Naomi grabbed him and gave him a big kiss right on the lips. Ernesto thought he was going to have a heart attack, but he didn't care. He would die happy.

"You're wonderful," Naomi sang, over and over.

It was just gratitude, Ernesto told himself. Nothing more than that. Just gratitude. Yet Ernesto had heard sentimental people say that, at momentous points in our lives, we can actually feel the earth move beneath our feet. Ernesto could have sworn the earth not only moved, but rocked back and forth.

Linda Martinez couldn't call Orlando on his cell phone until Thursday evening, after Felix had gone bowling with his friends. Every Thursday he went bowling with his friends from the *barrio,* and, while bowling, they had a few drinks. His wife prayed every Thursday night he didn't have too many to drive safely. Ernesto stopped by, at Naomi's request, to be with them.

Linda could hear the phone ringing. . . . Someone was answering her call.

"Orlando?" the woman said in a trembling voice.

"Mama!" Orlando shouted. He was a strong man, as strong as his father, as tough as his father, but his voice shook like a little boy's voice. He had not heard his mother's voice in three years. "Mama! Is it really you?"

"Yes, Orlando, are you all right?" she asked.

"Yes, Mama, yes," the son assured his mother. "I'm in Los Angeles now. I'm performing with a band. But I'll be back home to the *barrio* on the weekend. I'm playing there at the festival at Our Lady of Guadalupe Church. I'll be in town for several days."

"Orlando, Naomi has a very nice friend, Ernesto—" she began, her voice still trembling.

"Yes, I met him. I like him very much," Orlando interrupted.

"He said he will drive Naomi and me to meet you and Manny at a restaurant," Mama explained.

"*Maravillosa!*" Orlando cried. "We can meet at *Los Osos* in Old Town. It's a lovely place. When, Mama?"

"Sunday?" she suggested. "Next Sunday afternoon? I'll tell your father I'm visiting my sister. He won't suspect anything."

"It's on me, Mama, the whole dinner. Champagne for you and Martinelli's for Ernesto and Naomi," Orlando promised.

They finalized the arrangements and said their good-byes. Mrs. Martinez then put down the phone and looked at Naomi and Ernesto. "This Sunday. *Los Osos* in Old Town. He says it's nice. I cannot believe this is really happening. I have not seen Orlando in three years, Manny in less than that. I cannot believe I will see *mis niños* again, take them in my arms . . ." Tears rolled down her face.

Naomi walked over to her mother and gave her a big hug. Then Ernesto and Naomi went outside to play with Brutus. Brutus had been whimpering impatiently, waiting for someone to notice him.

After tossing a ball back and forth to the dog, Ernesto and Naomi sat on a stone bench in the backyard. The yard was beautiful, with climbing red roses and whimsical elves perched on plastic toadstools. There was a patch of green lawn and a koi pond. "Who did all this?" Ernesto asked. "Your brother?"

"No, my father. He loves to do yard work," Naomi answered.

Ernesto stared at the sly little elves, winking an eye. It was hard to imagine gruff, mean Felix Martinez designing such a display.

"Ernie," Naomi asked, "have the police got any leads yet about who threw the concrete through your window?"

"They haven't got back to us," Ernesto replied. "Could have been random vandalism, I guess. Couple months ago some creeps used BB guns to shoot out a dozen car windows for no reason."

Naomi was pensive for a moment. Then she said, "Ernie, I hope you don't, you know, think it was Clay. I mean he's got his faults, and he's ticked off and all that. But he'd never do something like that. He's no criminal, and that was a criminal act."

"I never really thought it was him," Ernesto replied, though the thought had crossed his mind. "I figured from the start that it was some gangbanger who didn't like my dad going around the *barrio* talking to kids. I thought the creep would be afraid

Dad would stumble onto some illegal activity, like drugs. I thought they wanted to scare Dad off from what he's trying to do. But they were wrong."

Brutus stirred and trotted over to Ernesto. Ernesto reached down and scratched his head. He seemed to like that.

"You know, Naomi," Ernesto told her, "Mom got to talk to the artist who's drawing the pit bull in her book. They were going back and forth on their computers, making changes and figuring out how the dog should look. It was great fun for Mom. I could just see the excitement in her eyes. This is the first really big thing that happened to her in a career kind of a way. Her parents thought she'd be a college professor or something, 'cause she was so smart in school. Then, when she didn't even go to college, they were disappointed. Mom's showing us a side of her now that we've never seen before, and it's good."

"I'm glad for her," Naomi remarked. "I think a woman should have a career. When

she's just a Mom and a housewife, sometimes she sort of doesn't have any power.
She gets to feel like a nobody. Like in my
house, Dad is always ending every discus-
sion with those famous words, 'I'm payin'
the bills, lady.'" Ernesto smiled at Naomi's
girlish attempt to sound like her gruff dad.

"And he is. He's generous with Mom,
but he always lets her know it's his money.
He doesn't mind if Mom and I go shopping
and bring home lots of bags. But in the end
it's his money and he's the boss, you
know?"

"It shouldn't be like that, Naomi,"
Ernesto objected. "My mom never worked
or brought home a paycheck. I guess she's
gonna get a nice advance for the book. But
that'll be the first money she earned on her
own since my parents got married. Still, they
got this joint checking account, and Mom
pays most of the bills. When they have to
decide about a big purchase, they discuss it
together. When the book is published,
though, wow, is she gonna be thrilled. Her

parents too. The other night Mom's mom called and sort of hinted maybe she should use the name Maria Vasquez Sandoval on the book cover. Mom talked it over with Dad, and he said whatever she liked was fine with him. Then Mom grinned and said, 'The name on the book will be Maria Sandoval, 'cause that's who I am.' " Ernesto's attempt to sound like his mother tickled Naomi.

"You know what, Ernie?" Naomi asked suddenly.

"What?" Ernesto responded.

"You're awfully cute, especially when you smile," she noted. Ernesto felt his face flush.

"I'm glad you guys moved back here, Ernie," Naomi told him.

"Me too," Ernesto agreed. "Well, gotta go home. I promised my father I'd help him find a phone. Like every five minutes, new ones are coming out with a zillion new apps. Dad's a great history teacher, but, when it comes to the new technology, I got him beat there. He's been wanting a new phone for a while, and he's looking for the best deal. He wants something voice acti-vated so he can dictate into it."

Ernesto headed home alone. He kept thinking about Naomi's words, delivered with such a gorgeous smile. Was she just being nice, or was she finding him more attractive?

When Ernesto got to the end of Blue-bird Street, he saw Clay's Mustang parked there. He was shocked and annoyed. Inside the car, Clay Aguirre was staring down the street at Naomi's house. Maybe he'd seen Ernesto and Naomi walk down the street together about thirty minutes ago.

Ernesto was tempted to walk over to the Mustang and ask Aguirre whether he knew that stalking was against the law. But he knew he might be just getting into an ugly confrontation that would solve nothing. So he tried to ignore Clay as he passed the car. But as he started to walk down Tremayne, Aguirre got out of the Mustang. "Hey Sandoval," he yelled.

Ernesto stopped and glared at the other boy, who came toward him. Clay was still bigger and stronger than Ernesto. But Ernesto had a lot more muscle now, and the outcome of any fight wouldn't be such a no-brainer for Clay. "Yeah, what's up?" Ernesto asked in an unfriendly voice.

"It ain't gonna work, dude," Clay warned him. "Just keep that in mind. You ain't getting my chick. You can try all you want. You can get ripped and gain weight. But some dude comin' here a few months ago and popping into Naomi's life, that isn't going to make her forget the eight years we had together. Turning on the charm and hanging around her house is just going to make her sick of you even faster. We're goin' through a bad time right now, but she'll come around."

Ernesto said nothing. He turned on his heel and walked along Tremayne Street toward Wren, with Clay still yelling at his back. "The guy's getting scared," Ernesto thought, "that's obvious. He knows he's losing Naomi. He's getting nervous. This smart girl's taken enough verbal abuse from him. She's finally wised up. She knows she's better than that."

On Sunday afternoon, Ernesto drove to the Martinez house to pick up Naomi and her mother. Zack was in the front yard, playing with Brutus. His mother didn't tell him about the visit with his older brothers. She wasn't taking any chances. Zack was pretty loyal to his father. He might just tell him, Mrs. Martinez thought, and she was terrified of the fallout from that. So Zack was told that Ernesto was driving his family to see mom's sister for a nice long afternoon visit.

"Say 'Hi' to Aunt Nina," Zack waved as the Volvo rolled down the driveway.

As they were going down Tremayne Street, Linda Martinez said, "This is so nice of you, Ernesto."

"No problem," Ernesto responded. Naomi was beautiful in a peasant blouse and dark jeans. She wore a turquoise necklace.

He had glanced at Naomi's mother when she got into the car. She was slim, and at one time she had been very pretty. She now looked very tired. The lines in her face were deep. She wore nice clothes, but she knew so little about fashion that she chose the wrong colors. She never found an attractive way to fix her hair; so it was simply tied in a bun at the nape of her neck. She wore lipstick, but nothing else on her face. Felix Martinez thought too much makeup made a woman look as though she was no good. Mr. Martinez was always faithful to Linda, but he was jealous of her when they were younger. He became uncomfortable when she wore clothes that were too pretty. That was why Naomi didn't try to help her mother look prettier by giving her advice on makeup and hair. Naomi didn't want to cause trouble.

Mrs. Martinez was obviously extremely nervous. She sat in the back seat, her hands clasped on her lap. But even though she held them tightly, they trembled. Naomi didn't sit next to Ernesto, as she usually did. She sat in the back seat with her mother, offering support with an arm around her mother's shoulders.

"It's been so long," Mrs. Martinez sighed.

"Yeah Mom," Naomi agreed.

"I'd almost given up that I'd ever see them again," the mother said, shuddering. "When Felix threw Orlando out, they were both like wild animals. It was so terrifying."

"Orlando looks really good," Ernesto interjected, trying to move the conversation to more positive things. "He sings great too. He did a solo with the Perez band, and he's almost as good as Oscar. I think Orlando is going places."

Suddenly Naomi let out a small gasp of surprise and dismay. "He's behind us!" she cried.

Linda Martinez screamed, "Not Felix! Oh! God help us!" Her eyes widened in terror.

"No, no, Mom," Naomi assured her quickly. "It's Clay Aguirre. He's been hanging at the house spying on me. He can't take no for an answer. I told him I didn't want to see him anymore, but he refuses to believe me. Now he's behind us in his Mustang."

"You should tell him you're calling the cops on him. They'll make him stop stalking you, Naomi," Ernesto snapped. "This is ridiculous."

"Oh no," Naomi objected. "I don't want to go that far. Just pull over for a minute, Ernie."

Ernesto pulled to the curb on Tremayne, and Clay parked behind him. Naomi got out of the car and walked back to the Mustang.

"Hey babe," Clay Aguirre greeted her.

"Clay, stop following us." Naomi's voice was sharp. "I mean it. I want you to leave me alone, okay? I'm not kidding, Clay. I'm asking you in a polite way now, but if you don't stop . . ."

Clay looked stunned. He looked at Ernesto, who had stepped from the Volvo and now stood alongside it in case Naomi needed help. Clay didn't say a word, but he made a U-turn and gunned the Mustang into retreat. In seconds he was gone.

When Naomi got back in the car, her mother said, "He calls the house all the time. He even asked me if there was something I could do to make you take him back. He's really in love with you, Naomi."

"I know, Mom," Naomi moaned. "But you know what happened. I've never had anybody hit me. It was so horrible that I had nightmares for days. Something changed inside me when that happened. I don't hate Clay. I could never hate him. I just don't feel the same way about him anymore, and I never could again."

Mrs. Martinez grew very quiet. She thought back to many years ago when she first started dating Felix. He was a handsome boy and very macho. All the girls were crazy about him. At the time, a very sensitive boy named Jaime liked Linda too. He wore glasses, and he was good in math.

Felix and his friends made fun of Jaime. He was a wonderful target. Felix's friends ridiculed him without mercy, and Linda remembered she laughed too. Boys expected their girlfriends to laugh at their antics. Even at that time it was very important for Linda to please Felix.

Jaime went on to become a doctor. Now he was married with four children and living in Texas. Sometimes Linda Martinez wondered what her life would have been like if she'd married Jaime instead of Felix. Linda was friends with the girl who eventually married Jaime. Her name was Emily, and even now the two families exchanged Christmas cards. In the photographs that came in the cards, Emily looked so happy there in Texas with Jaime and their children. They were always smiling and cutting up on their Christmas pictures. Emily didn't look like she was ever afraid of Jaime. Perhaps she was even the boss in the family, and he would be okay with that. He was that kind of a guy. He wasn't ever very macho.

Linda Martinez remembered to this day the first time Felix slapped her. They had been dating for about six months. He claimed she was paying too much attention to another boy. Felix called her bad names, and he slapped her in the face. Linda could still remember the salty blood in her mouth. After all these years, she still could feel the sting of pain.

Mrs. Martinez was aware that Clay Aguirre hit Naomi, and she wasn't too shocked. Clay was a lot like Felix at that age—very macho. A boy had to be macho, and sometimes that meant getting a little rough with a girl. Roughness only went to prove how much he loved the girl, didn't it? If Felix hadn't loved Linda back then, why would he have become so angry because she was smiling at another boy? And if Clay Aguirre didn't love Naomi, he would not have struck her in rage when she paid a compliment to another boy. Clay obviously loved Naomi. Linda Martinez wasn't sure whether Naomi was doing the right thing in ending their relationship. Turning away from so strong a love was a very big decision.

Linda clasped her hands even more tightly. If she had married Jaime, she didn't think she would be afraid so much—or maybe not at all. She looked at her beautiful daughter. With a sudden rush of love for the girl, she was glad that she had stopped dating Clay Aguirre. Naomi was right, she thought. When fear lurked in love, it was no longer love.

CHAPTER SEVEN

As they neared Old Town, Linda Martinez murmured in a small, sad voice. "They must hate me. I remember the last words Orlando spoke to me. Felix was throwing his possessions out on the front lawn. Orlando looked at me with those black eyes of his and he said, 'Mama, you're choosing him over me. Mama, how can you choose him over me? I'm your child.' He kept screaming that at me."

"It's okay, Mama," Naomi said consolingly. "Orlando understands. He doesn't hate you. He loves you. He and Manny want to see you so much."

Ernesto felt sorry for Mrs. Martinez. She had lived in anxiety and fear for so long that she did not know how to be happy, how to hope. She expected the worst. Ernesto glanced into his rearview mirror. Clay Aguirre wasn't following them anymore. Ernesto turned onto the freeway ramp. They would be in Old Town in no time. *Los Osos* turned out to be a two-story stucco building with a red tile roof. A series of wooden hitching posts for horses out front made it look like the old days. Ernesto pulled into the parking lot, got out, and opened the door for Naomi and her mother.

"I wonder if they're here yet," Mrs. Martinez said. "Maybe they changed their minds about coming."

"No," Ernesto protested, "they'll be here."

When they entered *Los Osos*, a girl in a flowing red skirt and embroidered white blouse welcomed them. A cheerful fire glowed over in the corner, and the walls were decorated with murals of Mexican subjects.

"We're joining two people who may be here already," Ernesto told the young woman. He glanced around and quickly spotted Orlando and Manny. Manny looked a lot better than when Ernesto had seen him on the street. He was clean and nicely dressed.

Naomi saw her brothers, and she put her arm protectively around her mother. "Mama, they're smiling. Over there!" she pointed. "Orlando and Manny are smiling."

Orlando and his brother jumped up and came toward their mother. "Mama! Mama!" Orlando cried, his voice thick with emotion. He was a big, strong young man, but now tears filled his dark eyes. He took his mother in his arms and hugged her for what seemed a long time. Then Manny did the same. Both boys towered over their mother's small figure. She had seemed lost in their arms.

"Oh Manny," Linda Martinez moaned, "you look so thin."

"He's gonna do better now, Mama," Orlando promised. "Tonight I'm taking him with me to LA. We're getting him a job working on the equipment with the band. Manny was always good at the sound system when he had that little garage band. Come on, sit down, sit down."

Naomi was standing nearby, her eyes bright with tears. She was overjoyed at how her brothers were welcoming their mother. Ernesto reached out and placed his arm around Naomi.

When everybody sat down, they ordered chicken *enchiladas* and *quesadillas*. Heaping dishes arrived, served family style, accompanied by rice and beans, corn chips, and *salsa*. Manny ate ravenously, making Orlando laugh. "He hasn't eaten in a year!" he chuckled. "Pretty soon he'll get big like me, eh?"

"Orlando," Mrs. Martinez said, "Naomi said you are a singer in a band. That was your dream when you were small. You'd watch the band from Veracruz. You even learned to play the *jarana*. Do you remember?"

"Yeah Mama," Orlando answered. "I sing with Oscar Perez. We do everything from traditional Mexican music to rock and roll. We want to be like *Los Lobos*. Oscar is getting some good gigs, and they're downloading our music on iTunes. Maybe we'll be in the big money, Mama,. Then I'll buy you a nice house in LA for you and Naomi and Zack." His eyes danced with excitement. "No more bowing and scrapin' to nobody, Mama."

Mrs. Martinez looked stricken. "Are you saying leave your father?" she asked.

"Yeah," Orlando responded. "You once needed him to support you, but if I made a lot of money . . ."

"Orlando," the woman chided, "he is *mi esposo*! For years he has taken care of me, of us. I could never leave him."

"Okay," Orlando suggested good-naturedly. "We won't talk about that now. Let's just enjoy the dinner and each other, eh? This is a big occasion, Mama. After all the rice and beans and chicken, we'll eat the heavenly *flan* they serve here."

Ernesto stayed out of the conversation for the most part. He loved Mexican food anyway. He just enjoyed that and the bubbling warmth among the family members. To him, it was beautiful that, after all the years of bitterness, the natural love among them would spring to life so easily. It was almost as if none of the bad stuff had ever happened. Ernesto wondered whether a time would ever come when such a dinner would include Felix Martinez as well. Was it possible he would be laughing and talking to his sons again? It seemed farfetched, but perhaps not.

At the end of the meal, the family hugged and kissed. And the boys promised their mother they would keep in touch. Eventually, Ernesto, Mrs. Martinez, and Naomi had to go to the Volvo for the ride home.

"I am filled with so many feelings," Linda Martinez mused. "I am so joyful and yet sad. I'm confused. These past years have been so hard. I am so thankful I have my boys again, but they don't understand my heart. I cannot turn against their father.

Never. I know he has hurt me. He has hurt me many times inside, but he loves me and I love him. I cannot be without him. I don't know any other way to be."

Ernesto dropped off Mrs. Martinez and Naomi at their house and then headed home. He felt happy about the day. He was so glad he could do this favor for Naomi and her mother.

When Ernesto got home, his mother was looking at photos of the illustrations for her book. The artist had sent electronic copies of them so that Maria could review them on her computer. "Look, Ernie, isn't Thunder cute?" she asked. "He's the dog in the story. Look at those eyes. Didn't Marc do a fabulous job? Marc's the illustrator. He's only in his twenties. He made our hero actually look lovable. And the cat—isn't that a cute face? She looks very wise too."

"Yeah, I like the pictures, Mom," Ernesto replied.

"Speaking of dogs, how is Brutus doing these days?" Mom inquired.

"Good, Mom," Ernesto answered. "I almost like the big guy. When he sees me coming, he's wagging his tail, all excited."

"They've had him neutered, right?" Mom asked.

"Oh yeah, absolutely," Ernesto affirmed. "That makes a big difference, Mom. The vet told Naomi and her folks something very interesting. Pit bulls, and even other aggressive big dogs, are three times more likely to bite people or other animals if they haven't been spayed or neutered. That's a big thing, you know. It's not just pit bulls that can be dangerous. A lot of big dogs are. Even German Shepherds and Huskies."

"It's so sad that a lot of people don't take care of their animals," Mom commented. "They let them breed and produce more unwanted puppies and kittens when the shelters are already bursting. Well, good for the Martinez family, that they took care of that. I suppose Linda had to beg Felix to get it done. I'd expect him to be dead set against neutering his pit bull."

"No," Ernesto said. "Actually he did it on his own. Zack told me his father checked into the breed and decided to schedule the neutering as soon as Brutus was old enough. Martinez seems like a stupid guy, but actually he's kinda smart about some things. He operates some real tricky machinery. It's a shame he's not nicer."

At school on Monday, Naomi had lunch with Ernesto. She asked him whether he'd like to come over to her house the next day after school and take Brutus for a walk. "I need to walk him, and I'd love to have you along," Naomi told him. "Then we can wind up at my house and have some of Zack's birthday cake. Mom baked an awesome *tres leches* cake for his birthday."

Ernesto was delighted by every chance he got to be with Naomi. "Sure, I'd love to," he responded eagerly. "Only it has to be after track practice. But I'll take the car to school and back. I just won't jog tomorrow."

Maybe his imagination was at work, he thought, but she *did* seem to be growing warmer toward him. She seemed friendlier every time they were together. Ernesto didn't believe in love at first sight. He believed in "like" at first sight, but love took a lot longer. You had to get to know a person before she really got into your heart.

The next day, Tuesday, Ernesto got home from track as soon as he could. He showered, put on fresh clothes, and left for Naomi's place. If records were kept for doing all that, he'd have broken them. Then Ernesto and Naomi set out with Brutus for a walk late on a balmy afternoon. As usual, Brutus was eager to go, but now the dog was better behaved. He used to tug and strain at the leash, but, as his puppy days receded, his behavior improved.

"Hey Brutus, old boy," Ernesto commented, scratching the dog on his head. "You're getting to be quite the gentleman."

"You know one of the reasons pit bulls have such a bad name, Ernie?" Naomi asked. "Gangbangers and other criminals buy them to guard their crooked dealings. Then they starve and mistreat them to make them meaner so they're better guard dogs. They leave them outside when it gets cold and rainy. It's awful."

They walked down Tremayne, past Ernesto's home on Wren Street. Then they passed Nuthatch where Carmen lived. Finally they got to Starling, where they turned for the trip back. The houses on Starling were not as nice as those on the other streets. The street had some foreclosures, and many of the houses were rentals. The absentee owners let their homes get rundown. When they got too bad, they had them torn down and built small apartment buildings. The lawns were brown, and there were no flowers. On Wren and Bluebird, beautiful jacaranda trees spilled their lovely lilac blossoms on the street. In the spring the whole street looked magical. On Nuthatch a lot of the people had flower gardens with roses and geraniums. On Starling Street, except for a few gawky Washington palms that looked like inverted broomsticks, there was no greenery.

"Look," Naomi pointed out. "The palm fronds droop, and no one trims the dead ones. Then rats and bats make nests in the dead stuff."

They were halfway down the street when Brutus started barking. He'd been happily sniffing tree stumps and shrubs when suddenly he became agitated. He looked alert and barked persistently.

"Something's bothering him," Naomi noted. "The other day some guy came to our door. He was supposedly selling cleaning products, but he looked suspicious. I think he wanted to see whether anybody was home so he could break in if the house was empty. Anyway, Brutus went crazy, like he sensed something wrong, like he's acting now."

They were in front of a small, rundown stucco house with burglar bars on all the windows. Old tires were stacked along one side of the house. A sign read "217 Starling" and contained a faded picture of a starling. Previous residents of the house must have put up the sign.

"Naomi," Ernesto remarked, "look, old building materials piled along the side of the house ... rotten wood, cement blocks ... looks like a dump. Hey, I see chunks of concrete like the kind that came through our window. I remember that chunk of concrete had red paint on it, and I see red paint on those chunks there too."

"Oh wow! Maybe . . ." Naomi said. Then her eyes widened. "Look, behind the chain link fence. Pit bulls!"

These pit bulls didn't look like Brutus. They were gaunt and bore scars. One of the dogs was missing an ear, and he looked as though he might have been used in dog fighting. The dogs were leaping up at the fence and yelping.

"Poor dogs," Naomi cried. "I'd be scared of them if they got out, but I pity them."

"That could be a drug house, Naomi," Ernesto warned. "They keep the dogs to scare people from investigating too closely." Ernesto reached down and patted Brutus on the head. "Good boy," he calmed him. "I have a feeling something ugly is going on in that house, maybe a *lot* of ugly stuff."

They continued walking to the end of the street where there were apartments. Yvette Ozono and her family lived in one of these units.

Yvette was in the side yard with her little brother and sister. She was helping them up and down the monkey bars. "Hi Ernie! Hi Naomi!" Yvette called out. When Ernesto and his father met her at Tommy Alvarado's funeral at Our Lady of Guadalupe Church, she seemed more dead than alive. Ernesto couldn't believe the difference in Yvette since she was back at Chavez. She had been like a sad zombie, but now she had come alive. Her face was usually bright with a smile.

"Hey Yvette," Ernesto responded, "there's a real ratty looking house down at the end of the street and I was wondering if—"

"217 Starling," Yvette interrupted him with a frown. "Yeah, they deal from there. They sell drugs and guns. Everybody's afraid of them. Guys with shaved heads, tattoos. Cars come and go a lot. When I walk to school, I go through the alley just so I don't have to pass the house. I told Mom we ought to call the cops, but Mom's afraid they'll get back at us. A lot of people feel the same way. They're scared to do anything."

"Thanks for the heads-up, Yvette," Ernesto said.

Ernesto and Naomi turned the corner with Brutus.

"Coulda been dudes from that house threw the concrete in our window," Ernesto suggested grimly. "Maybe they figured

Dad might've run across their dirty operations walking around the streets."

"Yeah," Naomi responded. "Are you telling your dad?"

"What do you think?" Ernesto countered. "My father works hard in that classroom. He puts his heart and soul into saving teens like Yvette and Dom and the rest of them. He's struggling—and guys like José Cabral are too—for the kids. It's like the good guys are filling the bucket from the top with pure clean water, and the creeps boring holes in the bottom."

"I hear you, Ernie," Naomi answered sadly.

"Everything my father and Mr. Cabral and the other good teachers and the good parents are trying to do, the scum in that house are trying to undo," Ernesto fumed.

Ernesto and Naomi went into the Martinez house to get some of the *tres leches* cake Naomi had promised. Zack had turned eighteen, and they had had a party for him and his friends last night. A few big slices of cake remained.

"Whoa, look at that cake!" Ernesto exclaimed when he saw it on the table. "Where did you buy that cake? Conchita's Bakery? She has the best."

"No," Naomi corrected him. "Mom made it from scratch. She always makes our cakes from scratch."

Ernesto sat down at the dining room table with Naomi and had a big slice of cake. It was the most delicious, most moist *tres leches* cake he had ever tasted. "Oh man, this is amazing," Ernesto commented, his mouth stuffed with cake. He saw Linda Martinez cleaning up some dishes, and he called to her. "Mrs. Martinez, I've never tasted such good cake. If you entered this cake in the county fair, you'd win the blue ribbon for sure."

Linda Martinez blushed a little, but she smiled. "Oh Ernie, that's so nice of you to say, but it's just a cake." She glanced over at her husband, who was watching television. He was also having a slice. Felix Martinez had heard what Ernesto said. Now he looked up.

"Yeah Linda, the kid's right. Cake is real moist ... real good ..."

When Ernesto got home, he told his father about the house on Starling Street. He told him about the gaunt, scarred pit bulls guarding the yard and about what Yvette had said. He described the chunks of concrete that lay alongside the house with telltale red paint on them. The more he said, the angrier Luis Sandoval looked.

"I'll talk to my friend at the police station," Dad promised. "In the meantime, don't walk there, Ernesto."

CHAPTER EIGHT

The next day, Ernesto, Abel, Dom, and Carlos were eating lunch at Cesar Chavez High School when Clay Aguirre walked by with Mira Nuñez. Clay didn't seem too into her, but she seemed to be delighted to be with him. Clay was a good-looking guy, and many girls were interested in him. Mira was feeling lucky, and she looked it.

Ernesto was afraid Clay was with Mira just to make Naomi jealous. He wanted to shake Naomi up. Clay glanced at Ernesto and his friends, and he seemed pleased that Naomi wasn't with them. Lately she'd been eating lunch often with Ernesto. Today, Naomi, Yvette, Tessie, and some other girls were eating together. The boys had lunch in a small, grassy ravine, and maneuvering Tessie's wheelchair down there would have been difficult. Anyway, Ernesto thought, girls sometimes want to talk girl stuff, and guys like him don't enjoy talking about the new fashions at the mall.

"The mural you guys made is ready, huh?" Ernesto asked Dom and Carlos. He'd watched the dramatic mural slowly develop on the side of the science building. Dom and Carlos, under the guidance of their art teacher, Ms. Polk, had drawn the design and made the outline. But many other students helped fill in the colors. The mural grew from a few splotches of vivid color to a very dramatic piece of art. When finished, it was a striking and poignant depiction of Cesar Chavez standing in the fields of grape vines, surrounded by the men, women, and children who labored in the fields. The mural showed the banner that Chavez always carried of Our Lady of Guadalupe and the symbol of the grape workers' union, the black eagle. Anyone approaching Chavez High would immediately be drawn to the beautiful mural.

All they needed to do yet was color in a little more blue sky. Then it would be ready for the unveiling ceremony scheduled for Friday. Local television news and reporters were coming from as far away as Los Angeles and the Sacramento Valley to cover the unveiling.

"We're gonna be on TV, man," Dom beamed, grinning. "You guys all bring your phones and take lots of pictures to post on the Net. My mom can't believe I'm part of something like this. I mean, she's always been hard on me. She always goes, 'You're nothin' but a lazy *bobo*.' And I guess it's been true, but now she sits up and takes notice. Her lazy *bobo* is gonna be famous!"

"Yeah," Carlos added. "My parents are blown away too. They're calling up all the relatives, the cousins they haven't talked to in ages. It's like I'm some big artist. They were so mad when I put graffiti on the fences. One time my old man whipped me for that. He said if he had to pay for cleaning up that stuff, he'd take it outta my hide. But now he's telling all his friends that his kid is like Diego Rivera or somebody."

"I'm glad for you guys," Ernesto told them. "My dad is so proud of you."

"Yeah," Dom admitted, "we were both ready to drop out of Chavez. Until he came up with this mural deal. Now I'm even acing math. I'm an official geek! Your old man turned us around, Ernie."

"But not everybody likes what he's doing," Carlos advised. "Lotta bad stuff going on in the *barrio*. Your dad shines a light where they want it to be dark."

Ernesto Sandoval felt cold. Lately his father was holding impromptu basketball games in the early evening. Teenagers were welcome. He had ice-cold sodas and chips. Dropouts were especially welcome. The games were another way for Luis Sandoval to get in touch with kids needing a push in the right direction, a way to redirect aimless kids. Ernesto's father was an All-American in basketball when he was a kid. He led his school to a championship. He still had the skills. He played under the lights now, and that wasn't the safest place in the *barrio*. The danger didn't lurk entirely in that house on Starling Street. Other gangbangers were out there. They had switchblades and guns. All Luis Sandoval had was courage.

Ernesto made a mental note to himself. He wasn't crazy about basketball, but it was okay. He enjoyed shooting some hoops once in a while. He decided that, when Dad headed over to Chavez to play, he'd convince his father that he wanted to go along. He'd say he needed the exercise. Ernesto wanted to be another pair of eyes watching for trouble. If he had his father's back, then playing in the evening might not be so dangerous.

On Friday after school, the television camera vans were lined up at Cesar Chavez High School. All the teachers and some council members were there. Many parents had also come. The art departments of several southern California colleges sent people. Ernesto saw his parents, *Abuela*, and his sisters arrive.

The wall mural had been draped with large curtain borrowed from the auditorium's stage. A podium had been set up with a microphone leading to PA speakers at both sides of the wall.

At designated time, State Senator Miriam Lopez stepped up to the podium to host the ceremonies.

"We hear so much in the media . . . ," Senator Lopez began and then paused until squealing feedback could be tuned out. "We hear so much about sad and negative things about our young people. But today we are here to celebrate a triumph of our community, our school, our teachers, and especially the students at this school. We will be unveiling a truly remarkable work of art that will inspire and beautify the school for decades to come. This wonderful mural was created by two young men from

Chavez with the help of their teacher and many other students who assisted in the project. The wonderful thing about this work of art is that it never would have happened at all except for the caring of our students and the dedication of our teachers."

Ernesto had spent some time the day before telling Senator Lopez how the mural came into being. She had listened attentively, and now Ernesto hoped she would give credit where credit was due.

Ernesto glanced over at the first friend he had made at Cesar Chavez High School, Abel Ruiz. When Ernesto was a stranger, Abel reached out to him. Right now Abel had a blank look on his face. He had no idea what was about to come. Tall, skinny Abel Ruiz, with a bad case of acne, shifted from one foot to the other, probably wishing the unveiling was over so he could go home. Ernesto smiled to himself. Abel was such a good friend. Ernesto loved the guy.

"It all began," Senator Lopez went on, "when one of our teachers here, Mr. Luis

Sandoval, identified two boys in his class. They didn't seem interested in studying or even in staying in school long enough to graduate. Their only passion seemed to be in graffiti. Yes, they were taggers. Well, they were talking to one of our juniors, Ernesto Sandoval, Mr. Sandoval's son, about how boring school was. Another junior, Abel Ruiz, heard about them."

Abel Ruiz snapped to attention. He looked shocked. He glanced at the senator and then at Ernesto.

"Well," the senator continued, "Abel Ruiz had a pretty good idea. The boys were graffiti artists, and they were bored in school. Maybe they could be interested in doing a mural for Cesar Chavez High School as colorful and dramatic as their graphic art on fences and walls of the community!"

Everybody was looking at Abel now, smiling. Abel's face got warm, but he was smiling too.

"Abel told his friend, Ernesto, and Ernesto told his father, Luis Sandoval. And a great idea was born. Two talented young men made a magnificent mural and decided maybe school wasn't so boring after all. And here is the result! Violá!" As she finished the presentation, the senator turned toward the covered wall.

The curtain dropped, and mural was unveiled to the cheers of an audience that had now swelled to several hundred. Television cameras rolled, and phones were aimed.

Senator Lopez began by thanking all the people who helped make the even happen. She thanked the students involved, the art teacher who supervised, and many others. She hoped she hadn't forgotten anyone.

Then the senator invited Luis and Ernesto Sandoval, Ms. Polk, Dom Reynosa, Carlos Negrete, and Abel Ruiz on stage to be acknowledged. As they were being introduced and applauded, Abel Ruiz hung back when his name was called. "I didn't do nothing," he protested. Ernesto grabbed his arm and pulled him onto the stage. Abel faced the cheering crowd with a nervous grin.

"The moral of the story," concluded Senator Lopez, "is that, when we cast a single stone into the water, the ripples go on forever, far beyond our ability to see them. Thank you, Abel Ruiz, for having a great idea. Thank you, Ernesto Sandoval, for carrying the idea forward. And thank you, Luis Sandoval, for making it happen. To Dom and Carlos and all of the other students who worked on this mural, thank you. It is the most beautiful piece of art in the whole *barrio*! May we all someday admire your work in the art museums of the world!"

The crowd of onlookers, young and old, loudly applauded and cheered. Senator Lopez stepped away, and the group on the stage began to break up. The TV news services moved in to buttonhole the politician and the other participants in the making of the mural. The next thirty minutes were spent in giving interviews for airing later that evening on TV.

The next Wednesday, Ernesto did not show up for work. He had gotten permission from his boss to take the night off.

Ernesto had to be at a track meet. The Wilson Wolverine fans filled their stadium to see the winningest track team Wilson High had ever fielded. Friends and families were ready to witness a romp over the hapless team from Chavez. As long as any of the students from Wilson had been in school, they had always soundly trounced Chavez. They didn't expect this afternoon to be any different. Wilson's Coach Amsterdam caught sight of Coach Gus Muñoz arriving with his team, and Amsterdam grinned and gave his boys a thumbs-up.

Coach Gus Muñoz been coaching for almost thirty years. Long ago, he had enjoyed some success, but that was before he came to Cesar Chavez High School. In East Los Angeles, where his boys had run like gazelles, he had coached a team to the regional championships. One of his boys even went on to win Olympic gold.

Muñoz was not young anymore. Ever since coming to Chavez, his record was dismal. He had always been a man with bad posture, even in the best of times. And a meet with Wilson had only made his shoulders slump even more. At the Wilson meets, he had been typically prepared for humiliation.

But not today. Deep in the man's heart, hope glimmered. He strode onto the field more erect, his shoulders as squared as they could be.

Avila was good. He was passionate about winning. Sandoval was good too. The others not so much. The chance of winning any of the races would all hang on those two juniors. Muñoz would consider it a miracle if they could take the relay. Still, Muñoz glanced nervously at the Wilson Wolverines, looking like a pack of cheetahs. Muñoz's shoulders slumped, but only for a moment.

Ernesto noticed that Clay Aguirre had come to watch the races. His new girl-friend, Mira Nuñez, was with him. Ernesto thought Clay figured Naomi would come to watch Ernesto run, and she did. Clay was hoping that Ernesto would thoroughly humiliate himself and that Naomi would be embarrassed too. That was why Clay had come. He was hoping to watch Ernesto drag the Cougars down to another defeat. When Naomi, Yvette, and Tessie in her wheelchair arrived, Clay looked happy. They would all see what a fool Ernesto Sandoval was. Clay's eyes followed Naomi as she pushed Tessie's wheelchair.

As Ernesto watched Clay, he wondered whether Mira noticed that her new boyfriend hardly ever looked at her. Didn't she see that all his attention was on another girl, the beautiful girl in the green pullover? Ernesto wondered when Mira would get wise to the fact that she was just a prop, a decoy.

Ernesto smiled and waved to the girls, and they all waved back. Ernesto thought that Naomi especially gave him a warm smile. He hoped that his imagination wasn't just working overtime.

Finally, the runners from both schools took their places at the starting line for the hundred-meter race. The favorite for this event was a lanky boy from Wilson named DeWayne Rodgers. He had won the event twice before, and now he was even stronger. Ernesto and Julio were also running in that event, and both were eager to win. As the boys got into their starting positions, Ernesto heard Clay Aguirre yelling, "Go DeWayne!" He yelled several times, until the Cougar supporters sitting around him threatened him with bodily harm. Clay didn't give a damn about the Chavez Cougars. He just wanted to see Ernesto go down.

When the starting gun went off, DeWayne flew from the starting line, as he always did, fully expecting to win. But both Julio and Ernesto were close behind him. Ernesto gave it all he had, but Julio pulled ahead of DeWayne to win the dash for

Chavez. DeWayne finished second and Ernesto third. For the first time as coach at Chavez High, Coach Muñoz had a joyous shock on his face. His guy actually beat Wilson! The small contingent from Chavez was screaming so loudly it seemed as though the stands were full of Cougars, not Wolverine fans.

Clay Aguirre was very pleased that Ernesto finished third.

Ernesto gave Julio a high-five. "You were awesome, man," he told him.

Julio grinned happily and, as usual, looked for his father, who was going crazy in the stands.

Julio Avila went on to win the two-hundred-meter as well, against two excellent Wilson sprinters. Julio was on fire.

Wilson boys had won the long jump and hurdles. But, if Cesar Chavez High School took the relay, the Cougars would have enough points to win the meet. As the relay teams took their places, Coach Muñoz's shoulders looked look a little more erect.

Jorge Aguilar was running the second lap, and Eddie Gonzales the third. Both boys had much improved over the start of the season, but they were not speedsters. Ernesto was determined to redeem himself by running the first lap so fast that taking the race would be a cinch for the others. So far Ernesto had not run his best for some reason. But the meet depended on the relay, and he wanted to make it happen.

As Ernesto eased into his starting position, he concentrated as he'd never done before. He remembered all he had learned about running, breathing, pumping his arms. This one lap would make him or break him today. He wanted to make it his personal best. He focused his mind on the one purpose he had before him: to complete this lap way ahead of the competition.

At the signal to go, Ernesto sprung into fluid motion. To those watching in the stands, he was a blur. Ernesto amazed himself by his speed. He seemed to burst into a whole other dimension. He heard gasps

153

from the stands, but he paid no attention to anything but his running. When he passed the baton to Jorge Aguilar, the handoff was smooth and flawless. Ernesto slowed down onto the grass, braced his hands on his knees, and sucked in large gulps of air. He didn't know it yet, but he had just run the fastest first lap ever recorded at Wilson High.

Jorge and Eddie ran well too, but neither came close to Ernesto's speed. Julio Avila would get the baton for the final lap with only seconds to spare. He could win his lap easily.

But nobody foresaw what happened next. A gasp of horror came from the Cougar fans when Eddie fumbled the baton while passing it to Julio. Julio lost precious time. He charged desperately into the final lap, arms pumping, his muscles stretched to the limit. Julio's father watched, anguish on his face. He believed the fumble had cost Chavez, and his son, the relay race. Most of the Cougar fans believed so too.

But Julio never believed so, and he never let up. Running the fastest he had ever in his life, he flashed over the finish line. As he did, the Cougar anchor seemed to be right beside him. Had he been he fast enough? He cooled down on the track with the other runners, walking in a tight circle, hands on hips, gasping for air. *Had he been fast enough?* The crowd was eerily quiet.

Then the announcement was made. The Cougars had won the relay! Julio had beaten the Wilson anchor by a heart-stopping two-tenths of a second. The Cougar fans were on their feet, shouting Julio's name: *Jul-i-o! Jul-i-o!* And then they started shouting another name: *Er-nest-o! Er-nest-o!*

Except for Ernesto's incredible speed during that first lap, Chavez would have lost the relay and the meet. Ernesto had blown the first lap into the stratosphere, giving the Cougars that slim margin of victory.

Julio and Ernesto embraced each other amid the wild cheers of the Cougar fans.

The only unhappy face among the Chavez section belonged to Clay Aguirre.

The meet over, a caravan of cars containing Chavez students traveled to Hortencia's restaurant for the victory celebration. Tessie rode in her parent's van along with Carmen. In the Volvo with Ernesto were Naomi, Julio and his father, and Abel. Behind them were five more cars filled with happy teenagers. As the huge group charged into the tamale shop, Hortencia threw up her hands and laughed, "It's an invasion!"

Before the celebration was all over, Hortencia suggested that Julio douse Coach Muñoz with a cup of nonalcoholic champagne that she brought from the back. The coach grinned happily as the champagne ran down his face and neck. "Now I can die happy," he announced, "but not before we win a bunch more meets and get to the regionals! I'm not retired yet!" The shop reverberated with the cheers of the crowd.

When finally Naomi and Ernesto were alone, going home, Naomi ordered, "Pull over, mister."

Ernesto pulled over to the curb and stopped. He looked at Naomi.

"Turn off the engine," she commanded.

When Ernesto turned off the engine, Naomi took his face into her hands and kissed him on the mouth like he had never been kissed before. "You were so great!" Naomi told him. "Not just because you ran that first lap like a champion, but for a whole other reason. I know how you've been training. I know how much you wanted to win the hundred meter and the two hundred. I could see the disappointment on your face when Julio beat you. But after both those races, you high-fived Julio like you were really happy for him. That took a real man, Ernesto. And then, after the relay, you could have hogged the glory 'cause we all knew that your amazing first lap won the relay. But you hugged Julio, and you were wonderful."

Naomi looked deeply into Ernesto's eyes. "I'm not sure what's happening to me right now, Ernesto. But something really strange is happening to me and . . . There isn't an earthquake going on is there?"

Ernesto was speechless. He felt as if he had been abducted by aliens and taken to an incredibly beautiful place ruled by a queen named Naomi. And she had, incredibly, asked him to be her king.

"I think I'm falling in love with you, Ernesto Sandoval," Naomi sighed.

Ernesto grabbed the girl and held her tight. "I love you too, Naomi," he whispered, unshed tears pooling in his eyes. "I've loved you for a long time. I've hoped and prayed that maybe someday you'd feel the same about me. But I didn't think it would ever happen . . ."

CHAPTER NINE

When Luis Sandoval went to play basketball that night, Ernesto tagged along. "You know what, Dad? I think I'll join you. I just feel like shooting some hoops tonight."

"You're not just trying to keep an eye on the old man, are you?" Luis Sandoval replied, a knowing grin in his eyes. "I can take care of myself, you know. After all the running you did at the track meet today, I wouldn't think you'd be up for hoops tonight."

"I used to like playing basketball, Dad," Ernesto protested. "I was never good enough to get on the team, but it's a nice warm night. I just feel like shooting a few baskets."

"Okay *mi hijo*," Dad agreed, looking unconvinced about Ernesto's reasons for tagging along. "It's always nice to spend some time with you, Ernie. So I'll take it. I love to be with my kids."

Ernesto and his father walked down the rapidly darkening street toward the basketball court. Usually six or seven kids showed up. Sometimes one of them would be a dropout, and Dad's eyes would light up at the chance to turn the kid around.

"When the baby comes, it'll be different at our house, huh Dad?" Ernesto asked. "It's been six years since we had a baby around. I was eight years old when Katalina was born, and then, when Juanita came, I was really excited. I guess it'll be fun having a baby around again. Mom is really excited. A baby and her new book. Man!"

Dad smiled. "I can't get over it. I never thought we'd get such a surprise gift. Just think of it, Ernie. When the child is in college, I'll be almost sixty! They'll think I'm the *abuelo*!"

"You'll be a great dad to the kid, just like you've been to all of us," Ernesto assured him.

"By then you'll be married, Ernie," Dad said, "with *niños* of your own. I hope my kids'll always be close. It's the way families should be. I am very close to Hortencia and Magda, Arturo, and Mario. We get together whenever we can. *Hermanos y hermanas*, they are so important in our lives. When our parents have gone, it is they who comfort us." Then he laughed. "Listen to me, I'm preaching to you as if already I'm a tiresome *viejo*!"

"Dad, it's real sad how it is with Naomi's family," Ernesto remarked. "Felix Martinez kicked the two older boys out. They had no contact until I took Naomi and her mom down to see them. Mrs. Martinez was so happy to see her sons, but she was scared stiff her husband would somehow find out. She kinda lives in fear all the time, but she always insists that she loves her husband and he loves her."

"A tragic situation," Dad agreed.

"Yeah," Ernesto went on, "but what's she gonna do? She had to decide if she would cut off the boys when they defied their father or break with her husband. That's a terrible choice. She's been married for almost thirty years."

"Well," Luis Sandoval suggested, "perhaps eventually Felix Martinez will relent and accept his sons back. When we get older, we sometimes realize that our stupid grudges are destroying us. The heart softens sometimes, Ernie. They are his sons. There is no stronger bond than between a father and his sons. Can Naomi talk to her father and ask him if he could ever find it in his heart to forgive his boys?"

"She kinda has done that," Ernesto answered, "and he always says the boys would have to apologize first. They'd have to ask forgiveness for what they did, especially Orlando. He hit his father, but he was protecting his mother. And he doesn't feel like he should apologize for that. I sorta don't either,"

The court lights were on, and some boys were already playing basketball when they arrived. As Ernesto and his father drew closer, his father suddenly remarked, "You've become very fond of Naomi, haven't you, Ernie?"

"Yeah ... yeah, Dad," Ernesto nodded yes. "I liked her from the beginning and the more I see of her ... you know, the closer I feel. She's pretty wonderful."

"*Mi hijo*," Dad said softly. "Something has changed. You're closer to her now than you've ever been. I can see it in your eyes, I can hear it in your voice when you speak of her. I know for a while she found it hard to break up with Clay Aguirre. But now I am feeling that she has and that you two have grown very close. Is that right?"

"Yeah, Dad," Ernesto admitted after taking a deep breath.

"Bear in mind, Ernie," Dad advised, "that if there is a future for the two of you together, the family will be in your life as well. Felix Martinez will always be a part of your life. You told me once that you felt contempt for the man, but that would have to change. You could not feel that way if the families came together. Your mother's parents had great dreams for her finishing college and having a fine career. Meeting me changed all that, and they were not happy with that. But they always respected me, and I always respected them. I think they are very good people, and I am blessed that my children have grandparents as fine as Alfredo and Eva Vasquez. Remember, Ernie, Naomi doesn't come without baggage. She will always love her father, and their family troubles will become your troubles."

Ernesto didn't say anything. All he could think about was that moment with Naomi after the Chavez Cougars won that track meet. She told him she was falling in love with him. She gave him a kiss that almost sent him into outer space. That was all that mattered now.

Luis Sandoval glanced at the four boys shooting baskets. "I don't recognize them," he said, as nodded in their direction.

"The one—the guy with the shaved head," Ernesto noted. "I saw him with another guy. He's the real bad dude who goes by the nickname Condor." His father nodded, finally having a face to go with the name he knew.

A cold chill went through Ernesto. He thought about the house on Starling and the half starved, maimed pit bulls. This guy seemed to be part of that action. On his thick muscled arms were tattoos of dogs. One of them looked like a rottweiler. Ernesto didn't know how bad this dude was, but he surely hung with an evil creep. Condor was about twenty, but this guy looked much younger, maybe not much more than fifteen or sixteen.

"Hey boys," Luis Sandoval called out, "you boys hot tonight?" Ernesto's father was wearing a Charger shirt and a black baseball cap. He looked a lot younger than he was. He could have passed for twenty-something.

"What's it to you, man," the rottweiler tattoo asked. He had a belligerent voice.

"I played basketball when I was a kid," Dad replied.

One of the other boys was a kid Luis Sandoval recognized as a sophomore at Chavez a few months ago. He declared, "Hey, you're that teacher."

"You're a teacher?" the rottweiler tattoo echoed the kid.

"Yeah, I teach history at Chavez," Luis Sandoval answered. "How many of you here are dropouts?"

The rottweiler tattoo and another boy raised their hands. The rottweiler tattoo spoke. "I didn't exactly drop out. I was like kicked out. But I did a little kicking myself before that went down." The four boys laughed at that.

"What's your name?" Ernesto's father asked.

"Tony," the boy responded. "I got suspended for fighting some creeps who were gonna take me apart and put me back together a whole different way. Like with my head comin' out my pants leg."

The boys laughed again.

"I'm Luis Sandoval," Dad announced. "This is my son, Ernie." Dad held out his hand to Tony, but the kid with the rottweiler tattoo declined it. Dad ignored the snub. "There's a lot about the school system that stinks. If some bullies jump a guy and he tries to defend himself, he gets busted along with the bullies. I don't agree with that Tony. If that incident happened to you as you say, maybe I can do something about it. Why should you lose your whole future just because some jackals came after you and you defended yourself."

Another boy chimed in. "He's jiving you, Tony. They're all the same. No teacher is gonna take the side of a kid who got busted for fighting."

"Yeah," another kid added. "He's the man."

"How old are you, Tony?" Luis Sandoval asked.

"Old enough to know a phony when I see one," Tony snarled. He was getting more hostile as his friends encouraged him. Teachers and cops were the enemy.

"How about I bet you I can make three free throws in the basket, and then you'll talk to me, Tony," Ernesto's father proposed.

"You can't do that," Tony protested. He folded his arms, and the rottweilers looked even tougher.

"He's jiving you, Tony," the other boy said again.

"Deal?" Luis Sandoval asked. Ernesto knew his father had been a great basketball player. In college, he had led his team in scoring. Most of his teammates were African American, and he was an oddity. He was the Mexican American kid who could shoot like Michael and Shaq. Now, twenty years later, Ernesto's father got together every year with his old teammates to eat hot dogs and pizza and to have a few one-on-one games.

"Waddya want to talk about?" Tony asked. "We got nothin' to talk about."

Luis Sandoval went to the fifteen-foot mark and shot his first ball into the rim.

"Big deal," Tony commented. "Beginner's luck."

Ernesto's father got his second free throw in and then the third. The four boys were dead silent.

"Okay, so you can play basketball," Tony granted. "But we got nothin' to talk about."

"You afraid to talk to me?" Ernesto's father asked.

"I ain't afraid of nothin'," Tony growled.

"Good, let's talk," Luis Sandoval suggested. He began walking to a stone bench nearby. The other three boys continued shooting baskets, but Tony stood there, a few feet from the bench where Luis sat. Then he walked a little closer.

"I'm tellin' you," Tony objected, "we got nothin' to talk about. I was busted. I'm done."

"How old are you, Tony?" Luis asked again.

Tony nodded toward Ernesto. "Same as him. I'm sixteen."

"Sixteen. I figured you were a junior," Dad replied. "You got a job, Tony?"

The boy laughed sharply. "Who's gonna hire me?"

"My boy there, Ernie, he's got a job at the pizzeria. You've worked at that pizzeria for about a month and a half, huh, Ernie?" Dad said.

"Yeah," Ernesto replied. "I make chump change, but it's better than nothing."

The boys who were still playing basketball stopped. They were staring at the boy standing by the bench where the teacher sat.

"I tried to get a job at a million places, the burger place, the taco shop," Tony revealed. "My parents were really ticked at me for getting busted. They said at least get a job, but nobody wanted nothin' to do with me."

"Because you're a dropout, son," Mr. Sandoval advised.

"I'm not your son," the boy snapped.

"Tony," Dad continued, ignoring the remark, "when a sixteen-year-old kid asks for a job, they want proof you're still in school. That tells them you're responsible. See, by being a dropout, you got a bad mark on yourself."

"So what? My homies take care of me," Tony argued.

"The bullies who stomped on you— they still at Chavez?" Ernesto's father asked.

Tony shrugged. "I guess."

"They straightened it out and got back in school," Luis Sandoval explained. "So now they're gonna graduate and get good jobs. It was their fault what happened, but you've been thrown under the bus. That's not right, Tony."

"It don't matter," Tony countered. "I'm doin' okay. There's a guy over on Starling gonna get me work."

Luis Sandoval and his son exchanged looks. "Guy named Condor?" Ernesto's father asked.

"So what if it is," Tony sneered.

"Tony, listen to me," the teacher demanded in a suddenly impassioned voice. "You're breaking your parents' hearts, and you know it."

"Ahhh, they don't care," Tony said.

"I bet your mama cries herself to sleep at night, worrying about her *muchacho*," Dad suggested. "The homies don't care about you. Condor just wants to use kids for his dirty deals. But a mama, she *always* cares. She can't help herself. She took care of you as an *infante*. That's what she remembers. That's what she never forgets!"

"What're you bothering me for, man?" Tony demanded in a suddenly distracted voice. "You crazy or something?" Tony looked at Ernesto. "What's with him? What's with your old man? Is he *loco*?"

"I want you back in school, Tony," Luis Sandoval explained. "I want you to be somebody. The kids in the *barrio*, they're the treasures here. That's what we're all about. The kids. I don't want to lose you, Tony. I don't want to lose any of you."

"You *are* loco, man," Tony declared. "I'm no treasure."

"Yeah, you are, Tony." Dad pulled out a card with his cell phone number on it. "You give this to your mama. Tell her to call me anytime. We'll work something out so you can get back in school. I promise you I'll help you, Tony."

Tony took the card. He could see the other boys were watching him. So he threw it down into the grass and yelled, "I don't need nothin' from you man!"

"Come on, Ernie," Dad said, "time to go home." He didn't say another word to Tony.

When they were several yards away, in the darkness, away from the lights, Ernesto spoke. "You tried, Dad. Most people don't even try. I'm proud of you."

Father and son stopped in the darkness. There was a crescent moon in the sky, and

Venus was creeping closer. Luis Sandoval watched the boys as their basketball game broke up. They drifted away, one by one, until Tony was left alone. Tony waited until they were all out of sight. Then he walked over to the stone bench where he had cast the teacher's card into the grass. He stooped and picked it up. He stuffed it into his pocket, and then he ran after his friends, who were down the street already.

"Dad!" Ernesto gasped. "He took the card with your phone number!"

Luis Sandoval smiled. "It's what I said about his mama that got to him, *mi hijo*. A Mexican boy cannot forget his mama. No matter how far from his home he is, he cannot forget that she loves him."

Ernesto and his father walked the short distance home. A few people on the street were getting out of the movie theater, coming from work, or going to work. A few kids were hanging out in front of the deli.

"You think he'll give the card to his mom?" Ernesto asked.

"Yeah," Dad nodded yes. "Probably not tonight. Maybe not even tomorrow. But soon."

"Do you think she'll call?" Ernesto asked.

"Yeah," Dad affirmed. "I wrote on the card in Spanish that I want to help the boy get back in school. Lotta these parents don't speak or understand much English. She'll call me. I know she will. They want what's best for their kids. They know it's school and a decent job, or it's places like Starling Street and friends like Condor."

The next day, Thursday, Luis Sandoval was very late coming home from Cesar Chavez High School. Ernesto watched *Abuela* and his mother putting dinner on the table, and they both looked worried.

"He usually calls when he's going to be late," Maria Sandoval commented. Worry underscored her eyes. Since that night when the chunk of cement came through the front window of the Sandoval house,

Mrs. Sandoval was much more concerned when Luis was late. Whoever had thrown that cement had meant to do harm. The thrower was probably angry about the teacher's activities reaching out to kids on the street and possibly uncovering drug dealing. Luis Sandoval had not curbed his activities, and the criminals who had done it had not been arrested yet. So Maria Sandoval worried.

"Luis must have been delayed at school. He has so much on his mind," *Abuela* said. "They're testing at the school now to see how well the eleventh grade is doing. Luis told me about that. He is maybe so busy with that that he forgot to call and say he would be late, Maria." *Abuela* was trying to comfort her daughter-in-law, but she was worried too. She almost dropped the bowl of salsa she was bringing to the table. She wouldn't have done that if she wasn't nervous.

"Where's Papa?" Juanita asked, her little face now dominated by her big, dark eyes. "Why isn't Papa home? He's *always* home now."

"Oh, he's just doing something at school," Katalina answered. "He's a very important man at Chavez High School. Ever since that pretty mural was unveiled, newspeople have been talking to him and stuff. Everybody knows that Papa is the most important man at that school, even more important than Ms. Sanchez, the principal. She wouldn't know what to do if Papa wasn't there to help her all the time. *Everybody* knows that." Katalina tossed her head in her self-important way.

Ernesto knew his father's routine. He always stayed in his classroom for about forty-five minutes to an hour after his last class ended. He wanted to be available in case a student needed to talk to him, about schoolwork or anything else. As much as Luis Sandoval loved teaching history, he loved even more his interaction with students, being able to help them through tough spots.

By the time Ernesto's father usually left the campus, it was pretty deserted. Only one other teacher, José Cabral, the math teacher, and Ms. Hunt would be there an hour after the last bell. Their three cars would be in the parking lot, and they'd hail each other as they finally left.

"Probably somebody came in to talk to him," *Abuela* suggested. "You know how he is about that. He's always willing to listen to a student. He has such a good heart."

Abuela chopped the salad. She knew her son walked down dangerous streets and challenged the gangbangers. She was proud of him. He didn't let fear cripple his life. But she was worried too, a little more with each passing minute.

"Mama!" Juanita yelled. "A car is coming in our driveway, and it's not ours!" Ernesto saw his mother's eyes widen. They all rushed to the window, almost afraid to see who had come.

CHAPTER TEN

It's Daddy!" Juanita screamed. "Some lady brought him home!"

Maria Sandoval looked out the window, smiling with relief that washed over her like soothing warm water. "It's Ms. Sanchez, the principal of his school, honey."

Dad waved to Ms. Sanchez as she backed out the driveway. He looked very tired when he came through the front door with his briefcase, but he looked happy too "What a day," he sighed. "It's like the start of that novel by Charles Dickens—*A Tale of Two Cities*. It was the worst of days, it was the best of days." He walked over to his easy chair and collapsed into it while *Abuela* got his favorite drink, hot chocolate.

"What happened?" Mom asked. "Where's our minivan?"

"Water pump problem," Dad responded. "I was going to walk home, but Julie Sanchez took pity on me and drove me. Pepe at the garage picked it up. He's fixing it and bringing it over tonight."

When Luis Sandoval sat down to dinner with his family, he told his story. "At lunchtime I got a call from *Señora* Valverde. That's the mother of the boy, Tony, that Ernesto and I met the other night. She spoke fairly good English, and she was distraught. Very emotional. Very frightened. She told me her son had given her the card for offering to help him get back in school. She wanted to know if it was something real or a joke. I assured her that, if she was Tony's mother, we needed to talk. Fortunately, I had a free period after lunch."

Dad paused while he munched a forkful of his dinner. "So I went over there. The old minivan's water pump hadn't burst, yet but it was dripping. *Qué suerte! Señor* Valverde was home too. It seems they are both nurses at the hospital. They work long shifts and they are struggling to raise four children. It turns out *Señor* Valverde had served in the same sector of Iraq I did, and he lost an eye to an IED. The parents told me that Tony was a good boy who was mercilessly taunted by a little group of boys. He was a B plus student."

"What happened, Dad?" Ernesto asked.

"Tony's a bit shorter than most juniors," Dad explained between chews, "and these bullies focused on this. They called him demeaning names. They just wouldn't let up. They scrawled stuff on his locker. In the lunchroom they overturned his tray and splashed spaghetti all over him. The more they did, the bolder they got until the poor kid snapped."

"Didn't the boy get help from a teacher or the principal?" Mom demanded. "This is despicable. It shouldn't be happening."

Ernesto looked sympathetically at his mother. She was young yet, not even forty.

So her high school days were not that far back. Yet she didn't understand how it was, especially for boys. Girls froze out their enemies and played mean little mind games, but boys meant business. You got bullies on your case, and they were like a pack of wolves sensing vulnerable prey. They didn't quit until they had brought you down. And you didn't rat them out even then, because then the whole class would be against you.

"He couldn't talk about it, Mom," Ernesto said to her. "You go crying to a teacher, and you're road kill."

"Well," Luis Sandoval went on, "Tony struck back. When these four creeps tore up the back of his brand-new Chargers jacket, a gift from his dad on his sixteenth birthday, he'd had enough. It turns out Tony Valverde wasn't the wimp they thought he was. He banged up these bullies and had them backed up against the wall. The irony is, he came out looking like the bad guy. The creeps got off with detention, and Tony got suspended. He was fighting on campus, and Ms. Sanchez threw the book at the kid."

"Can anything be done?" Ernesto asked.

"You bet your life," Luis Sandoval replied with a sharp grin. "Julie Sanchez and I had a long, *long* talk about what really went down there. Clearly, the administration was asleep at the switch while bullies were torturing this kid, and he ends up the scapegoat. I told Ms. Sanchez that we all dropped the ball here, and that we've got to make it right. I told her the kid is very bitter about what happened. I told her he's throwing in with real bad dudes and his life is going down the drain. Ms. Sanchez promised me she'd take the appropriate steps. In her defense, she'd tried working with the parents at the time. But she didn't get them to respond much. Her guess was that they were uneducated people. For some reason, they seemed afraid of dealing with someone in authority, like the principal."

"Dad, that's amazing!" Ernesto remarked. "You're the bomb, Dad."

"Well," Luis Sandoval wagged his head and smiled right at Ernesto. "I kind of have you to thank for the way it all turned out, Ernie. Remember when Dom Reynosa and Carlos Negrete were giving me a hard time in class? They were saying they didn't like their boring old history teacher. You told them about my Iraq experience. I was kinda miffed at the time. I don't want to use my tour in Iraq to hold sway, but that sure did change the way Dom and Carlos looked at me."

Dad shoveled some rice and chicken into his mouth. "Mmm! Mama? Maria? Whoever cooked tonight is a queen of the kitchen!"

"Hunger is the best sauce," *Abuela* said, grinning happily that her son was home and at his dinner table.

"Anyway," Dad continued, "what you told them kind of helped me get through to those guys. We were able to keep them in school to do that mural. Hey, I thought while I was talking to Julie Sanchez, *mi hijo* is a pretty clever guy. Well, Julie was hemming and hawing. Oh, how hard it would be to get Tony back in class after he'd been busted for brawling on campus. So I happened to mention that the boy's father is a war hero. He was a young guy who went overseas to defend his country, and he paid a real big price. He lost an eye and suffered serious scarring on the left side of his face. This guy won a Purple Heart and some other medals."

Another forkful of *arroz con pollo* disappeared into Dad's mouth. "So," he continued, as he munched, "I told Julie Sanchez that's what Guillermo Valverde did for his country. So maybe the school could cut the kid some slack. All he was doing was defending himself against a pack of jackals that the school couldn't control. She changed real fast. Her tune was very different."

Abuela clapped her hands. "*Viva mi hijo!*" she cried. Katalina and Juanita joined

Ernesto in applauding while Mom added music by beating on the table.

The next day at school, Ernesto decided he would ask Naomi Martinez for a date— a real date. It was time. A new 3-D movie was out that everyone was raving about. The special effects were supposed to be amazing. Ernesto and Naomi had talked about it, and they both wanted to see it.

Ernesto skipped lunch with his friends in the usual place and went looking for Naomi. He found her at the vending machine trying to decide between an apple, a pear, and an orange.

"The pears are awesome," Ernesto commented.

"Yeah?" Naomi responded. "They look beautiful. I love pears when they're just right. Not mushy, but crisp. That one in the slot looks good."

"Go for it!" Ernesto urged. His heart had begun to pound. He was pretty sure this was the time to make a real date. Naomi gave every indication that she was warm to the idea, but Ernesto still doubted himself.

Naomi put her coins into the slot and reached into the compartment for the pear. "Ohhh," she sighed, taking a bite, "it's perfect!"

"Naomi, uh," Ernesto hesitated, "you doing anything special Friday night?" His attack of the nerves got a little worse. He focused on how she'd kissed him in that special way. That kiss had to mean something. She even said she thought she was falling in love with him. Maybe those were just hollow words, spurred by the excitement of the moment. Maybe she'd thought about her words later and regretted them. But Ernesto was going to give it a shot. Ever since that kiss, ever since those beautiful words, he could think of little else but Naomi.

"I don't think so," Naomi responded. "Why?"

"You know that movie we were talking about?" he reminded her. "The one with the awesome special effects? It's playing at the mall, and I thought I'd go see it Saturday night. It'd be great if you could make it too, you know. I mean, we could get pizza or something after, whatever you'd like. And, you know, they say the thing is a real experience and if you're not busy with anything else, I just thought . . ." Ernesto ran out of breath.

"Yes," she replied.

"Yes?" Ernesto gasped.

"Yes, I want to go, silly," Naomi giggled.

"Okay then, gr-great!" Ernesto stammered. A big grin spread across his face. For the rest of the day and rest of the week, Ernesto walked on a cushion of air, not on the campus of Cesar Chavez High School.

That Saturday night, as they drove to the multiplex theater at the mall, Naomi made an announcement. "My dad was in a really good mood last night. He just got a raise at work. His boss told him he was the best guy they ever had on the heavy equipment. The boss, whom Dad calls '*bobo estupido*,' really went up in Dad's estimation. So I grabbed the opportunity. I dragged out some old photo albums of long ago when we were all little kids. I showed Dad me and my brothers playing on the slides and the monkey bars. At first Dad had kind of a weird look on his face. He even looked mad. Then he got nostalgic, which isn't normal for him."

"What did he say?" Ernesto asked.

"Well, he starts talking about him and Mom wanting kids right away when they got married. But they'd about given up when Orlando was born. Dad grins and tells me how happy he was to have a son, then two more sons, and a daughter. Then he leans back in his chair, and he goes, 'What happened? It was so good back then. Why did those boys go bad? Did I do something wrong?' "

"Your dad said that?" Ernesto asked, with an unbelieving look on his face.

"Yeah!" Naomi answered. "Usually he right away blames Mom for being too easy on my brothers. But last night he wondered if he made some mistakes. So I get really nervy. I ask him what he'd do if Orlando showed up at the door right now."

"What'd he say?" Ernesto asked as he drove into the parking lot at the mall.

"He goes, 'Orlando ain't never gonna show up around here,'" Naomi went on. "And I say, 'But what if he did? Him and Manny too?' And Dad looks at me and says, 'You don't ever forget your kids, even if they hate you and you hate them. You don't never forget them.'"

"Man!" Ernesto exclaimed, as he parked the Volvo and put on the parking break. "Maybe, just maybe he's softening up a little. You need to call Orlando and tell him. I mean, years ago I read something in a history textbook. This tough Israeli guy, Begin, he meets up with this tough Egyptian guy, Anwar Sadat. The two countries were at war and hated each other. But they made a peace treaty, and Israel and Egypt stopped being enemies. That happened with two tough old politicians after years of hatred and war. So maybe your dad and his boys could make peace too."

Naomi laughed. "Yeah, I think I'll call Orlando and tell him what happened. It would make Mom so happy if our family was whole again. It'd make me happy too. And even though he'd never admit it, I think it would mean the world to Dad too."

A lot of people were in line at the theater. The movie had created a big buzz. Finally Ernesto and Naomi got to their seats, their 3-D glasses on. Then the movie started. At first, they spent some time ducking the 3-D missiles coming off the screen toward them. When scenes got very scary, Ernesto put his arm around Naomi's shoulders, and she snuggled up to him. The movie lived up to what Ernesto expected and then some. Any movie that got Naomi close to him was all right with him. For that reason alone, the movie was a big winner.

After the movie they stopped for pizza in the mall. They both liked pepperoni and lots of cheese.

"You know," Naomi remarked as the pie was served, "I don't ever remember having as much fun on a date as I did tonight."

"Me too," Ernesto concurred. To himself he said, "I'd have fun watching paint dry if you were beside me watching it too."

As they headed home in the car, Naomi made another comment. "Clay hasn't given up. He texts me all the time. I'm polite to him, but I'm answering him less and less. I hope he and that Mira get closer. Then maybe he'll forget about me." Naomi turned serious then. "You know what, Ernie? If it hadn't been for you, I'd probably still be with Clay."

Ernesto stiffened. He wasn't sure what she meant. Did she regret that her long relationship with Clay had ended. "Yeah?" was all he said.

"Yeah," Naomi went on. "It's so weird. I've just never before been close to a guy like you. You can be very masculine, even macho when you have to be. But you can be sensitive and compassionate, and really sweet at the same time. You do that in a way that just melts my heart." Ernesto would have been very content if Naomi had stopped talking at that point.

But she went on. "I love my dad, but he's rough and harsh a lot of the time. And my brothers . . . Orlando can be as tough as Dad, and Manny is so weak. Zack just goes with the flow. Then I met Clay. He could be so romantic and nice and very macho. I liked him a lot, but he put me down all the time. He thought he was funny, but he hurt me. He did it often enough that I found myself being careful about what I said and what I did. But I thought, hey, that's the way guys are. I'd never really known any other kind. If you wanted a man—a strong man—you had to put up with the bad stuff. Then, of course, he hit me, and that was too much. But I still needed the courage to end something that had been in my life since middle school."

Ernesto's head was spinning. She started by talking about a guy who's sensitive and compassionate and sweet even though he's masculine and a little macho too. Ernesto had thought she was talking about him. Now he wasn't sure. He was silent, trying to figure out where he stood with Naomi.

Just before they reached their part of town, Ernesto stopped the car for a red light. In the dark interior of the car, Naomi turned to Ernesto and spoke softly. "I never knew a guy like you existed, Ernie." She smiled and ran the back of her soft hand down his cheek.

"Babe," she sighed, "you showed me something I'd never known before, something I've always wanted even though I didn't know how much I wanted it. You gave me the courage to do the right thing—to break from Clay before I ended up in a world of hurt. Thank you for that."

Ernesto's doubts blew away like so much smoke. He wanted to hold her tight at that moment. But then the light turned green, and he had to go.

Still, this was just possibly the most amazing, wonderful night of his life. He didn't want this night to end—ever. He wanted it to go always.

As they neared their neighborhood, suddenly the best night of Ernesto's life turned ugly. Up ahead, near where they lived, he could see the flashing lights of police cars and emergency vehicles. As ecstatic as Ernesto was just seconds earlier, now he felt stark terror. Something had happened in this neighborhood, near where his family lived.

A million thoughts sped through Ernesto's head—all of them bad. "Oh man!" he blamed himself. "While Naomi and I were at the mall enjoying the movie, something big was going down around here. Is my family okay? Did something bad happen, maybe worse than a chunk of concrete coming through the window? Was it gang warfare? A shooting? Were people hurt or killed? Did someone attack our house? Is my family OK? Is Dad OK?"

Ernesto drove over to Bluebird Street to drop Naomi off. She had turned the car radio on and was hitting the scan button for some local news. A terse voice was reporting a police operation on Starling Street. The whoop of a siren and other voices could be heard in the background. A meth lab and a cache of guns and ammo were found. Three gang members were in custody. One of them was Condor.

Ernesto pulled into Naomi's driveway. All seemed well at the Martinez house. They embraced for a long moment. Naomi knew Ernesto needed to get home. Then he left.

Ernesto was numb by the time he reached his driveway. But all seemed OK. When he came into the house, his father smiled at him. "I just called the Valverdes," Dad said. "Tony is safe at home. If we hadn't talked to him, he might have been in that house on Starling tonight. Did you hear about that raid? We saved him, *mi hijo*."

Then Dad added one more thing. He'd called his friend on the police force. His friend wasn't on duty but told Dad about a major no-knock raid on 217 Starling Street. Dad reported on part of the conversation.

"Do you think any of them were responsible for the concrete coming through our window?" Dad had asked his friend.

"Probably, Luis," the police office responded. "But nobody's going to waste time on a vandalism charge. These guys are looking at dealing, weapons possession, maybe even money laundering. They were really connected. Even if we turn them to get at the bigger dealers, they'll have to go into witness protection. It was a really big operation for such a small town, Don't worry, Luis. Your windows are safe from now on."

Ernesto gave his father and mother big hugs. It had been a good night—a beautiful night. Ernesto would remember this night for as long as he lived.

Shortly afterward, the excitement had died down. The family members were all finally ready to try getting some sleep. Ernesto went down the hallway to his room.

Lying in his bed in the dark, Ernesto noted that the night was quiet again. It was also far less frightening. His dad, Mr. Luis Sandoval, had shown no fear. Street gangsters had sent a clear sign that he was in danger. But Dad kept doing what he needed to do. What he thought was right to do. And he won that staredown. Not only that, he'd saved Tony Valverde from destroying himself.

"My dad's a great man," Ernesto almost said aloud, alone in his room.

Ernesto also thought about Mrs. Martinez. Perhaps someday she could live as Dad does. She'd taken a big step by meeting with her sons. But she still chose to live in the shadow of a bully and abuser.

"Someday," Ernesto hoped, as he drifted off to sleep, "she will live with no fear too."